"*Why not come home with me?*"

Kyle traced a tantalizing line across Ashli's lower lip with a teasing finger. "We can talk there."

Back to the bachelor's lair, Ashli thought drily. Kyle Hamilton was rumored to have women's hearts for breakfast. "No, thank you."

He raised an eyebrow. "Running away? You still have a very low opinion of me, Ashli."

"I never said that."

"You don't have to. I can read you like a book."

Ashli practically choked. "I don't have to listen to this."

"Well, then," came the caustic reply, "better run on home, little girl. You wouldn't want the big, bad wolf to get you!"

Dear Reader,

The festive season is often so hectic—a whirlwind of social calls, last-minute shopping, wrapping, baking, tree decorating and finding that perfect hiding place for the children's gifts! But it's also a time to pause and reflect on the true meaning of the holiday: love, peace and goodwill.

Silhouette Romance novels strive to bring the message of love all year round. Not just the special love between a man and woman, but the love for children, family and the community, in stories that capture the laughter, the tears and, *always,* the happy-ever-afters of romance.

I hope you enjoy this month's wonderful love stories—including our WRITTEN IN THE STARS selection, *Arc of the Arrow* by Rita Rainville. And in months to come, watch for Silhouette Romance titles by your all-time favorites, including Diana Palmer, Brittany Young and Annette Broadrick.

The authors and editors of Silhouette Romance books wish you and your loved ones the very best of the holiday season . . . and don't forget to hang the mistletoe!

Sincerely,

Valerie Susan Hayward
Senior Editor

VICTORIA GLENN

Too Good To Be True

Silhouette Romance

Published by Silhouette Books New York

America's Publisher of Contemporary Romance

For Johna Machak

SILHOUETTE BOOKS
300 E. 42nd St., New York, N.Y. 10017

TOO GOOD TO BE TRUE

ISBN: 0-373-08837-X

First Silhouette Books printing December 1991

Printed in the U.S.A.

Books by Victoria Glenn

Silhouette Romance

Not Meant For Love #321
Heart of Glass #362
Mermaid #386
The Matthews Affair #396
Man By the Fire #455
One of the Family #508
The Winter Heart #534
Moon in the Water #585
The Tender Tyrant #628
The Enchanted Summer #652
Second Time Lucky #718
Life with Lindy #813
Too Good To Be True #837

VICTORIA GLENN

comes from a family of writers. She makes her home in the Connecticut countryside, but divides her time between the East and West coasts. She considers it essential to the creative process to visit Disneyland theme park at least twice a year.

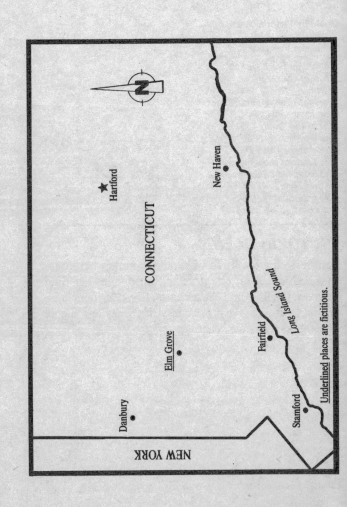

Chapter One

It was a long drive from the Arizona desert to the town of Elm Grove, Connecticut. The film of dust and dirt, which coated Ashli Wilkerson's beloved yellow pickup truck, bore testament to four days on the road. Her usually bright hazel eyes were dulled from weariness. Her vibrant brown hair wilted against her shoulders, and every muscle in her supple, young body ached from endless hours in the driver's seat. But in a few minutes, she thought with relief, the exhausting journey would at last be over. Just a little bit farther up the winding country road and Ashli would see the familiar driveway.

Home.

An involuntary smile flickered across her sun-tanned face. Home, to a refreshing shower and a de-

liciously firm mattress. Home after a six-month
absence. At the moment, the idea of being back in the
soothing serenity of home was rather appealing. All
Ashli wanted now was some peace and quiet.

The grimy old pickup rounded the next curve.
"What the—" She stared through the streaked wind-
shield in disbelief. The tranquil country lane was con-
gested with an endless parade of parked cars. Ashli
pursed her lips ruefully and steered the truck into a
huge circular driveway. She joined a procession of
automobiles discharging their elegantly attired pas-
sengers. Even now, scores of women in glittering evening gowns and distinguished gentlemen in tuxedos
were ascending the marble steps of the rambling Tudor mansion.

Oh, terrific! Ashli shook her head in utter resigna-
tion. Just wonderful!

A sharp voice jolted her. "Hey, lady," shouted one
of the red-jacketed parking valets, gesturing impatiently. "Guests only in the front...deliveries in the
back!"

"What?" she asked, surprised.

"You heard me," the young man snapped. "Deliv-
eries around the back!"

If she wasn't so exhausted, Ashli might have found
the energy to laugh. Instead, she merely gave a weary
sigh, and turned off the engine. She reached across the
torn seat for her knapsack, pulled the keys from the
ignition, and jumped down from the cab.

"Listen, lady—"

"No, *you* listen," she said, her voice quiet but firm. "I *live* here." Ashli ignored the stunned expression on the parking attendant's face and trudged up the driveway toward the house. Numerous guests stared at her with overt curiosity. Her wrinkled, faded khaki shorts and tank top were glaringly inappropriate attire. Well, who cares, she thought with a faint smile.

To say the least, finding herself in the middle of another one of Helene's glamourous soirees wasn't Ashli's idea of the perfect homecoming. She wondered what on earth *this* particular party was all about, then stopped herself. Since when did her sister ever need a reason to throw a party?

As she climbed the front steps, the gentle musical strains of a small live orchestra filtered toward her. The tinkling of glassware and sounds of laughter grew louder. The massive oak front door had been propped open, and in another moment, Ashli found herself in the crowded entry hall, surrounded by scores of well-dressed party guests. *Be it ever so humble,* she thought with a sigh.

"Miss Ashli!" a familiar voice exclaimed.

"Hi, Charles," she said, grinning happily at the plump, middle-aged man in a butler's uniform. Dear, wonderful Charles. He'd been around forever, it seemed. Since before she was born. If she hadn't looked so dingy and he hadn't been so dignified, Ashli probably would have hugged him.

Charles unceremoniously set his champagne-laden silver tray down on the sideboard and stared at her with undisguised delight. "Your father will be so pleased to see you!"

"I hope so," she responded. "I didn't tell anyone I'd be coming." Ashli stared around the crowded entry hall with obvious apprehension. "As usual, I suppose my timing was a little bit off."

"Don't worry, Miss Ashli," he said. His cool, usually formal voice took on a gentle tone. "In the matter of your homecoming, anytime is the right time, I assure you." Without missing a beat, he reached assertively for the battered knapsack. "Please permit me to bring your luggage upstairs while you . . . mingle." He paused. "Would you care for some champagne, Miss Ashli?"

She shook her head and watched in silence as the butler proceeded up the circular staircase, carrying the mud-stained canvas bag as if it contained diamonds. Well, Ashli thought philosophically, at least one person was pleased to see her home.

"Well, honestly!" The sharp voice belonged to a beautiful regal-looking blonde. "This is so typical of you!"

"Hi, Sis!" Ashli affectionately embraced the slender, exquisitely gowned young woman. "Miss me?"

Helene brushed her sequined dress disdainfully. "Ashli, you're a mess!"

"*You* look gorgeous, of course."

"I'm beginning to think you enjoy embarrassing me! What do you suppose my guests are thinking when my own sister strolls in looking like she's been shipwrecked on a desert island!"

"How was I supposed to know you were having another one of your fancy parties?"

Helene's lovely blue eyes narrowed in exasperation. "If you called Dad and me once in a while, maybe you might find out what was going on in this family."

Ashli shifted uncomfortably from one sneakered foot to the other. "Ah, well, I meant to call, but things got really hectic."

Helene crossed her arms. "In other words, there weren't any telephones in the middle of nowhere, as usual. And what obscure archaeological site were you and those egghead friends of yours unearthing *this* time?"

"It was an ancient Indian pueblo, dating back to—"

"Please, spare me! I'm sure it was every bit as thrilling as the one last summer in Peru, and what was that place the year before that? The one with the old bones of those dinosaurs?"

"Mastodons." Ashli sighed good-naturedly. "It was the Black Water Draw in New Mexico, and it's a fascinating study in early American culture. Did you know that the museum there was able to preserve some of the first-known examples of man's ability to domesticate animals?"

"Like I *really* care!" her older sister whispered harshly. "You look like something the cat dragged in, Ashli! For goodness' sake, run upstairs and put on something presentable before you completely humiliate me!"

Ashli ignored the remark and glanced around the cavernous entryway. "Where's Dad? I want to surprise him."

"Oh, you'll surprise him, all right! Would you please go upstairs and change your clothes first!"

"Change into what, Helene?" came the teasing response. "I haven't got a thing to wear!"

"Fine, go ahead and be a brat!" The other woman's tone was scathing. "Go ahead and ruin my engagement party."

Ashli stopped dead in her tracks. "Your *what?*"

"You heard me."

Utterly astonished, she stared at her older sister. "Your *engagement* party? You mean to tell me that you're engaged to some guy and you never called to let me know?"

Helene shrugged irritably. "You didn't have a telephone, remember?"

"You could have written!"

"I don't write letters. I could break a nail."

Ashli shook her head with amazement. "My big sister is getting married. I can't believe it!" If she hadn't already known how much it would annoy Helene, she would have given her another hug. "Well, I suppose congratulations are in order. Who's the lucky man?"

There was a pause. "Kyle Hamilton."

"*Who?*"

"You heard me."

If a bomb had exploded at her feet, Ashli could not have been more astounded. "Kyle Hamilton! You've got to be kidding!"

"Keep your voice down!" Helene whispered. "For heaven's sake, somebody might hear you!"

Kyle Hamilton, of all people! She had been away from home for just six months, and the entire world had gone mad. How could her sister even *think* of marrying such an egotistical, arrogant, superficial character? Ashli hesitated and gazed at Helene intently. "Whose idea was this, Helene?"

"The party?"

"No, not the party. This *marriage.*"

For the slightest instant, Helene's lip actually trembled. "It . . . it was mutual."

"Do you love him?"

"Love?" came the brittle retort. "What does love have to do with anything? It's an overrated emotion, believe me!"

Ashli felt a sudden stab of pain inside her own heart. Certain wounds were still too fresh not to sting. "If you aren't in love, why on earth are you getting married?"

Helene gave a thin smile. "Because it's the sensible thing to do."

"That's a reason?" A knowing expression finally crossed her face. "Wait a minute. I think I see Dad's fine hand in all of this."

Nervously, Helene checked the exquisite jeweled watch on her slender wrist. "Kyle and I will be making the official announcement in less than ten min-

utes. Could you at least run a comb through your hair
and put on some makeup? This is an important evening for me.''

"Sure," Ashli said, sighing, "I can see how giddy
with happiness you are."

In a rare sisterly gesture, the other woman touched
Ashli's shoulder. "One day you'll see. You'll understand that there's no such thing as love. Not really."
Without waiting for a reply, Helene turned and walked
down the hallway and into the bright, noisy living
room.

Ashli stared after her mutely. Helene and Kyle
Hamilton! Incredible. If there were ever two people
who were more ill-suited to each other, it was Kyle and
Helene. Even at thirty, there was something childlike
and vulnerable about her sister. At the same time, she
remained cool and repressed, with an odd kind of
brittleness.

Ashli had always been the outgoing, popular one.
She might have been pretty, with her hazel eyes and
mischievous smile, but there was no way she would
ever possess the astounding perfect blond beauty of
her older sister. The one thing she did possess that
Helene never would was a sense of humor. At this
moment, however, Ashli found little humor in the situation.

It was obvious that this little engagement had been
cooked up by the heads of the two most powerful
families in Elm Grove—Andrew Wilkerson and Jonas
Hamilton. It made perfect sense. Hadn't her father
always dreamed of just such a grand alliance? And

hadn't his old crony, Jonas, also entertained the same hopeful dream? The fly in the ointment had always been the elusive, unwilling bridegroom, Mr. Kyle Hamilton. Mr. Perfect Everything. Perfect blond hair. Perfect smile. Perfect athlete. And the most unbelievably large ego in the entire world. Ashli groaned inwardly. Poor Helene. How would she ever be able to tolerate life with a man like that?

By this time, the entryway was empty and still. It was evident that all the guests had begun to assemble in the main living room. With a resigned sigh, Ashli ran a self-conscious finger through her wilted hair and decided Helene was right. She'd better go upstairs and freshen up. She trudged up the winding, gray-carpeted staircase. Her muscles ached with every step.

Finally, she was back in the familiar pastel pink and green of her own bedroom. More than anything right now, Ashli wished she could just flop down on the antique four-poster bed with its fluffy pink quilt and sink into the delicious oblivion of sleep. But an announcement was about to be made downstairs, and she had an obligation to her sister. Even if Ashli knew in her heart that Helene was making the biggest mistake of her life.

Of course, Ashli thought cynically as she trudged toward the bathroom, *she* was probably the last person on earth to give anybody else advice when it came to matters of the heart. It hadn't even been a week since her own romantic illusions had been forever shattered. That was the real reason she had finally realized that remaining in Arizona was impossible. That was the real reason she had taken off so abruptly and driven home. But how could she ever admit to her father and Helene that Dr. Edward DePaul, the most wonderful young archaeologist in the world—the man who had been her idol since she had entered the university—had broken her heart? And the sad part was, that he would never know how she felt about him. To the absentminded Professor DePaul, Ashli Wilkerson had been just another enthusiastic graduate student. Edward would never be aware of the pain his impending marriage had caused her.

Oh, what was the point of even *thinking* about it! Angrily, Ashli turned on the gleaming chrome faucet and splashed ice-cold water on her face and neck. Then, she buried her face in a velvety, mint-green towel. Well, at least some things never changed. Ashli had forgotten how luxurious it was to have one's very own bathroom. The glistening porcelain and the mirrored glass of the shower and vanity table had been kept shiny and dust-free as if she had never been away. From the silver shell-shaped dish filled with French-milled soaps to the delicately embroidered matching pastel fingertip towels, everything familiar seemed to welcome her home.

Quickly, Ashli brushed some of the dust from her hair and surveyed her image in the mirror. Helene was right, she did look like something the cat dragged in. Her loose-fitting khaki shorts and tank top were hopelessly wrinkled. But she would have felt ludicrous and hypocritical were she to change into her fancy evening gown right now. Besides, there wasn't enough time. Stubbornly, Ashli decided that she would wear what she was wearing now, and if people didn't like it, that was too bad. She brushed the excess dust from her shorts and headed back through the bedroom and out into the corridor. This whole dumb marriage arrangement is ridiculous, she thought angrily. Helene was going to be utterly miserable. Ashli chastised herself as she bounded blindly down the staircase. Maybe it was partly her own fault for not staying in touch with her family. Sure, she and Helene had never been very close, but perhaps if Ashli had known about the situation sooner, she might have been able to talk her sister out of making such a terrible decision.

Ashli was so immersed in her reproachful thoughts that she was completely oblivious of something tall and massive standing at the base of the stairs.

"Oh!" was all she had time to exclaim before tripping headlong into a hard, tuxedo-clad chest.

"You ought to drive more carefully around those turns!" a deep voice remarked, while a pair of strong arms steadied her on the last step.

"I'm sorry," Ashli murmured and looked up at the man who had broken her fall. The bright blue eyes, which crinkled with laughter in the corners, and the dazzling white smile could only belong to one person. How absolutely embarrassing! "If it isn't Kyle Hamilton," she remarked.

The elegantly clad gentleman stared at her, puzzling out her identity. "You're Ashli, aren't you?"

"That's right." Strangely uncomfortable, she pulled away from his warm grasp. "I'm surprised you've got such a long memory."

He crossed his arms thoughtfully. "Oh, I've got a pretty good memory. The last time I saw you must have been when you were just starting high school."

"Gee whiz, I'm just *so* impressed," Ashli shot back scathingly. Back when she'd been a teenager, all her girlfriends would sit around the swimming pool at the country club and moon over Kyle Hamilton. It was devastating to admit that even she hadn't been immune to his charm. Of course, back then, she'd been a plump, mousy changeling. No man had even noticed her. It was hard to believe that Kyle Hamilton was telling the truth when he'd said he remembered her. "I find it highly unlikely that you would remember me after all these years," she said, pursing her lips. "You never noticed me before."

He eyed her steadily. "Noticing and remembering are two separate things. Wouldn't you agree?"

She was momentarily stunned. "Kyle Hamilton, are you actually saying something cerebral?"

He barely flinched. "Don't you think I'm capable of some degree of depth?" came the quiet inquiry.

"I wouldn't have any idea," she shrugged. "I hardly know you."

"Quite true. In fact, you don't know me at all."

Something in his perfectly chiseled face unsettled her. A kind of tension Ashli had never noticed before. "Well," she said, clearing her throat nervously, "in any event, I understand congratulations are in order." She extended her hand with almost forced politeness.

He looked at her penetratingly. "You obviously don't mean it, so why bother?"

Stunned, Ashli drew her proffered hand away. It was a shock to realize that Kyle Hamilton had the sensitivity to so accurately gauge her feelings. "I'm sorry if I've offended you." The apology seemed torn from her lips. His gaze continued to disturb her.

"I'm not offended." Now he seemed to hesitate. "I understand you're studying to be a scientist."

"Who told you that?" She was surprised that the man knew any detail about her at all.

"Your father mentions it often. He's very proud of you." He paused. "It seems to me rather unscientific to formulate an opinion on another person based upon hearsay."

She met his astonishingly intense blue gaze head-on. This was hardly the kind of conversation Ashli had ever expected to have with Kyle Hamilton, of all people. "Do you really believe that I've prejudged you?"

"Yes," he replied simply.

"I'm sorry," Ashli responded again, but this time, her apology was genuine. Perhaps she had misjudged him all these years. Maybe there was a real person underneath the carefree playboy image, after all.

"I have an excellent idea," he said, his mouth twisting in faint amusement. "Let's do away with all preconceptions, and pretend we're both meeting each other for the first time, right here and now."

"I beg your pardon?"

"You heard me." The devastatingly attractive man in his perfectly cut tuxedo extended his hand and clasped her own in a firm shake. "How do you do, Miss Ashli Wilkerson? I'm Kyle Hamilton."

Ashli smiled despite herself. "How do you do, Mr. Hamilton? Pleased to meet you."

"The pleasure is all mine, I assure you."

There was such obvious sincerity in his tone that Ashli was momentarily nonplussed. And what was this strange sensation in the pit of her stomach? No, Ashli thought hastily. She had to be imagining that.

"Ashli," he said, still holding on to her hand. "It makes me feel incredibly old when you call me 'Mr. Hamilton.' "

"Hmm," she shot back with forced playfulness. "Exactly how old are you, anyway?"

"A good deal older than you."

Yes, Ashli mused. How old was the man now? He had always seemed so grown-up, even when she was a child. Thirty-four or thirty-five would be a pretty accurate guess. "You make yourself sound like Methuselah."

This time, the dazzling smile did not reach his eyes. "I'm more than ten years older than you." With a sudden awkwardness, Kyle Hamilton released her hand from his warm grasp. "I'm practically another generation, Ashli."

"I suppose," she agreed, shrugging indifferently.

"In any event, I wish you'd call me Kyle."

She regarded him curiously. "It's the least I can do, Kyle, since you're practically a member of the family." This time, her smile was heartfelt. "I can't very well go around calling my future brother-in-law 'Mr. Hamilton,' now can I?"

A shadow briefly flickered across his taut, handsome features. "Quite right."

At that precise moment, Ashli knew instinctively that something was wrong. Very wrong. "Kyle," she began tentatively. "About my sister. She deserves to be happy."

There was an uncomfortable stillness. "Everybody deserves to be happy," Kyle said quietly, "but I believe there's no such thing. Inevitably, happiness eludes us all. One needn't be a scientist to figure that out. It's simply a fact of life." And with those cynical words ringing in Ashli's ears, Kyle Hamilton turned abruptly, and walked toward the brightness and laughter of his engagement celebration.

Chapter Two

Ashli would never forget the incredibly strange events of the night before. When she awoke, having slept late into the following afternoon, it was still hard to believe that her sister's elaborate engagement party hadn't actually been some bizarre, surrealistic dream.

Having just been informed of Ashli's unexpected arrival, Andrew Wilkerson had burst into the empty hallway, red-faced and beaming. "I wondered what it would take to get my baby home," he said, embracing his younger daughter joyfully.

"Hi, Pop."

"Don't you 'hi pop' me!" the distinguished, silver-haired gentleman retorted in mock annoyance. "Showing up at the last minute like this! One would think you didn't care about your own family!"

"Oh, I care."

"Hmmph!" Her father took another puff of his imported cigar. "Well, I must say you have a strange way of showing it. Six months and not even a phone call."

Here we go again, Ashli thought. "I wrote letters," she said.

"Letters!" he retorted disdainfully. "A father likes to hear his child's voice every now and then, you know."

She put her arm around his shoulder affectionately. "Well, I'm here now. Sorry if I'm underdressed for the occasion."

Andrew Wilkerson grinned broadly. "Leave it to my adventurous daughter to make everybody else look like overdressed nincompoops. Anyway, the important thing is that you're here to share this wonderful moment with your sister."

Ashli's expression was troubled. "About this *wonderful* moment. I get the distinct impression it's more wonderful for you and Jonas Hamilton than it is for Helene and Kyle."

The wealthy industrialist coughed, trying to evade his daughter's closer observation. "Nonsense! What ever gave you such an absurd idea?"

His daughter gave a thin, knowing smile. "You two arranged the whole thing, didn't you?"

"I cannot possibly imagine what you mean."

Ashli refused to budge. *"Dad."*

Her father began to look distinctly uncomfortable. Helene had always been the obedient, sensible daughter. But it was his younger child who had never been intimidated by Andrew Wilkerson's formidable presence and personality. She had always been precocious and uncowed. Even as a youngster, Ashli had possessed the uncanny ability to see through her father's well-meaning lies and subterfuges. "So, all right," he conceded gruffly. "Perhaps Jonas and I helped move things along, just a *little*."

Ashli sighed. "Oh, Pop."

"Don't look at me that way! I'm only thinking of what is best for your sister. You must admit that she and Kyle make a stunning couple. Just like two movie stars. What gorgeous grandchildren I'm going to have, huh?"

At that moment, Ashli realized that her father was in no mood to listen to any arguments or objections to his grandiose schemes. He had achieved the crowning ambition of his life—to unite two small empires into one large empire. And if at the moment the prospective bride and groom didn't seem particularly delirious with joy, that was just a minor detail that would be ironed out in time. Ashli shook her head in defeat. "Helene isn't in love with him. You're aware of that, aren't you?"

Andrew Wilkerson stamped out his cigar in an empty crystal champagne glass. "Are you trying to give your father a headache?"

She continued to challenge him. "Without love, what is the sound basis for a happy marriage?"

"You want to know? All right, I'll tell you. There is no sounder basis for a long and happy marriage than business. Add to that, the ties between two fine families with many interests in common.''

''But what about love?''

''Yes, what about love? As long as we're on the subject, how kind has love been to *you*, my dear? How happy has love made you?'' When he saw the way his words had made Ashli flinch, his harsh expression softened. ''Trust me, sweetheart, I know what I'm talking about. I've been on this earth a good deal longer than you. I've seen what a terrible price love can exact on the human heart. It's never worth it.''

And that was her father's final word on the matter. The subject was now closed.

On the stroke of eight o'clock in the evening, a strangely subdued Helene and Kyle stood by the grand piano, beneath the glittering Viennese crystal chandelier. After the two radiant fathers-in-law-to-be made their joyful announcement, the hundreds of guests applauded with wild enthusiasm. Then, everyone raised their glasses for the traditional champagne toast.

''Have you ever seen such a perfect couple?'' Ashli overheard one elderly guest exclaim to her companion.

''Just like the cover of a magazine,'' the man said.

Ashli felt compelled to agree with them. The glimmering light from the elaborate chandelier reflected off Helene's sequined silver evening gown and diamond jewelry. Kyle's short blond hair seemed to glow with Helene's like bright gold.

Golden, thought Ashli. That's what the two of them looked like. *A golden couple.* Well, who knows, maybe there was a chance for this marriage, after all. Stranger things had happened in the world. Perhaps, for all his cynicism, her father was right. Maybe Helene and Kyle would turn out to be well matched.

Just then, there was a drum roll from the band, and Kyle Hamilton placed an exquisite five-carat diamond engagement ring on his fiancée's manicured finger. There was more wild applause. Helene seemed to revel in the warmth and adulation of the spotlight. Her normally pale cheeks grew flushed, and her blue eyes positively sparkled. She raised up her slender, bare arm and held out the magnificent bauble for everyone to see and admire. But what Ashli found puzzling was that never once did her sister glance in the direction of the man she was going to marry. It was as if Helene was standing alone on a vast stage, savoring her moment as the center of attention. Perhaps Ashli was just tired, and her imagination was working overtime, but there seemed to be something contrived and artificial about the entire scene. Was she the only one to notice that although the future bridegroom nodded and smiled vaguely at the assembled crowd, there was an almost imperceptible tension in the lines of his handsome face?

But for all her awesome powers of observation, the one thing Ashli did fail to notice was the fleeting expression of regret in Kyle Hamilton's weary blue eyes as they came to rest upon her, his glance completely undetected.

* * *

When at last she sat up in her bed, Ashli reveled in the familiar surroundings of the room that had remained unchanged since her childhood. This was quite different from waking up every morning in a tent. But though she was relieved and happy to be home, part of Ashli's heart still remained out in the Arizona desert.

It was the excavation of the pueblo that had been the source of her hurt and trouble. Ashli had served as an unpaid volunteer at the digging site for the past two months. At first, she had been like everyone else on the team—thrilled and delighted when Dr. Angelique Boulez, one of Europe's most prestigious archaeologists had expressed an interest in the project. But when the renowned scientist turned out to be a sensual redhead with a bewitching French accent, it became quite a different story.

For five years, Ashli had loved the brilliant yet boyish Professor Edward DePaul from afar. Every summer, since her freshman year at the university, Ashli had signed up to work with him on his various field projects. Even in the blazing sun and heat, it had always been an inexpressible joy to work alongside her soft-spoken mentor. Edward, in turn, had come to treat her as a close friend and confidante. Surely, in just a matter of time, she would become more than just a friend. Edward was a very shy person, and all Ashli needed was patience. So she had thought. But then, Angelique arrived at the site and the sparks that instantly flew between herself and Edward were all too obvious. And finally, last week, the two archaeologists happily announced to everyone at the camp that they would be getting married in the fall. For Ashli, the news had been simply too much to bear.

It took thirty minutes beneath the strong spray of a steamy shower to purge those painful thoughts from Ashli's mind. That was the real reason the party last night had seemed so contrived. When she had watched her sister and Kyle, she had been remembering how Edward and Angelique had been so obviously in love, unable to take their eyes off each other for even an instant. But between Helene and Kyle there had been no sparks, no excitement. Their faces had been completely devoid of the radiance and anticipation of a couple truly in love. It was a stark, bitter contrast.

Ashli stared at her smooth, tanned face in the foggy mirror as she brushed the tangles from her wet, brown hair. Maybe, if she had been blond and beautiful like Helene, Edward would have taken his friendship with her a step further. She surveyed her delicate features for another moment, with a critical frown. Oh, sure, there had been some young men in school who had told her she was pretty. Certainly, when she bothered to put on a little makeup and wear something other than baggy shorts or old dungarees, Ashli herself had to admit that she didn't look half-bad. Still, there was a difference between simply being attractive and possessing the stunning, breathtaking beauty of Helene, or Angelique Boulez. Men practically gasped each time either of these two women entered a room. Ashli could not imagine what it must feel like to have such

blatantly strong female power. Dejectedly, she pulled
her damp hair back into a tight ponytail. Then, she
seemed to hear her mother's voice talking to her as a
little girl. "Try to think of one good thing you have.
Just one." Well, she shrugged now at her reflection in
the mirror. At least she had naturally long eyelashes.
That was something. Sure, it was superficial, but at
least, it was *something*.

The rambling Tudor mansion built by Andrew
Wilkerson was a tribute to years of hard work and
sacrifice. As a struggling young shopkeeper, he had
singlehandedly transformed his family's small hard-
ware business into the largest retailing chain in the
Northeast. He was already forty years old by the time
he finally married, and began a family. His wife, Rita,
had been a soft-spoken young woman nearly half his
age. It had been a bitter blow when she had died after
a short illness, leaving the grief-stricken Andrew to
raise two small daughters, aged five and eleven.

Of his two children, Helene had been the quiet, un-
demanding one. She had never made any trouble.
Ashli had always considered her older sister a regular
goody-two-shoes. She, on the other hand, had always
been getting into one scrape or another. To put it
mildly, Ashli had always been noisy, mischievous and
high-spirited...a genuine problem child. It wasn't until
she had gone away to college that she seemed to find
contentment and tranquility.

The transformation was largely a result of having
left the stifling atmosphere of Elm Grove far behind.

This former farm community in the heart of the rolling Connecticut countryside had become quite the trendy getaway for upscale urban professionals. The chief industry in the village now seemed to be real estate sales. And most of the real estate was under the control of the wealthy Hamilton clan.

Fifty years ago, the Hamiltons had been a well-established farming family. Now, their holdings made them even richer than the Wilkersons—a fact that Jonas Hamilton took great delight in constantly reminding his boyhood chum, Andrew Wilkerson. The two men had spent their entire adult lives in good-natured competition.

Now, as she prepared to go downstairs, Ashli seemed to remember some of the conversations she had overheard years ago between the two men.

"You can't take it with you, Jonas," her father had said, grinning at his old friend over a glass of scotch as they sat in lounge chairs by the country club swimming pool.

"Well, Andy old man, you can sure do the next best thing!" came the confident challenge.

"And what's that?"

"Keep it in the family. Always keep it in the family," Jonas Hamilton had declared.

"You might have a point," her father had remarked thoughtfully. "I'll go you one further, though. Why don't we keep the money in *both* families. How old is that handsome boy of yours?"

There was a roar of laughter from the other padded lounge chair. "I can read your mind, Andy."

"One day, when my Helene is old enough—"

Jonas nodded his head approvingly. "One day, when Kyle finally sheds his wild ways and decides to settle down—"

Ashli recalled that she had only been eight or nine years old, sitting with her feet dangling in the wading pool when she'd overheard the two men's plans. Strange, how adults never thought children heard or understood their conversations.

"Miss Ashli." A cultured voice jarred her back to the present. "I've taken the liberty of preparing you a late luncheon."

Ashli thrust her hands into the pockets of her faded jeans. "Thanks, Charles, but I'm not very hungry."

The butler stood below her on the carpeted staircase, his stance resolute. "Hungry or not, you haven't eaten anything since your return last evening." There was reproof in his tone.

"I'm almost twenty-four years old," she reminded the man plaintively. "I scarcely need a mother hen!"

"Yes, Miss," came the cool reply. "A simple chicken sandwich, fresh fruit salad, and milk is waiting for you on the terrace." Without another word, the butler turned and walked down the winding staircase.

Ashli watched him go with a mixture of affection and amusement. The plump, balding Charles had been the closest thing to a mother that she had known since the age of five. Seldom smiling, the exceedingly proper British houseman had seen Ashli through bouts of measles and chicken pox, made sure her shoelaces were properly tied, and year after year had tended to

scraped knees, runny noses, and mismatched hair
ribbons. One thing Ashli had learned after all these
years was that there was no arguing with Charles
Wingate. If she didn't go downstairs right this minute, and eat the meal he had so meticulously prepared
for her, she would suffer the frigid glare of Charles's
disapproval all day.

A few moments later, Ashli was comfortably seated
on the patio, picking idly at the corners of her sandwich. In the distance, she could see Helene dressed in
a short, blue summer dress, walking across the green
expanse of lawn with a young man Ashli didn't rec-
ognize. The two of them appeared to be engaged in an
animated conversation. Curious, Ashli watched as her
sister and the young man came closer to the house. As
they drew near, she wondered who this stranger was.
He was built like a beanpole, had shaggy brown hair,
and wore a pair of ragged, paint-stained white dungarees. He seemed intent on saying something to Helene, and she, in turn, seemed to be listening with rapt
interest. Suddenly, Helene threw back her head and
laughed. It was a light, spontaneous sound. Ashli was
mystified. She had never seen her sister behave in such
a relaxed and carefree manner.

A moment later, the young man turned and walked
away across the back lawn. Helene watched him go,
and then strolled slowly toward the terrace.

"Who was that?" Ashli asked.

"Oh, nobody," Helene answered vaguely.

"*Nobody,* huh?"

"Don't look at me like that, Ash!" her sister demanded.

"How am I looking at you? I just asked an innocent question!"

Helene shrugged her shoulders. "His name is Simon, all right?"

"Simon what?"

"How should I know? He's working next door on a natural rock waterfall for the Henderson's swimming pool." Her sister paused. "He's really an artist, though."

"I see," Ashli said, staring at her sister in fascination. It was so very unlike Helene to take an interest in any man who didn't wear a suit and carry a briefcase.

"It's not what you think!" Helene glared indignantly. "Simon happened to run into me when I was having brunch with Doralee Henderson this morning. He's a sculptor, and he thinks I have outstanding bone structure."

"Mm-hmm." Ashli nodded as she toyed with her spoon. "Just remember, Sis. You're an engaged woman."

The older woman stamped her foot. "Oh, for heaven's sake! Do you really think I would ever be interested in a starving artist who lives in a trailer? I'll bet Simon doesn't even own a tie!" There was a pause, as Helene looked at her younger sister. "It's just that he wants me to pose for him."

Ashli's jaw dropped. "Without your clothes on?"

"Certainly not!" Helene seemed scandalized. "Simon wants to do a bust of me, with my hair upswept like that ancient dead Egyptian queen…what was her name?''

"Nefertiti. She was the wife of King Ikhnaton in the fourth century, B.C.''

"Whatever,'' Helene said, waving her hand dismissively. "The point is, I'd appreciate it if you didn't mention this to Daddy or Kyle. They might get the wrong idea.''

Ashli shrugged. "Why would I mention it to them? It's nobody's business but yours, believe me.''

He sister smiled with relief. "Thanks, Ash. It's just that they might not understand that it's all in the name of art.''

"Oh, I understand completely,'' she said, nodding solemnly. Well, why not? It might do Helene some good to loosen up and expand her intellectual horizons a little before she married Kyle Hamilton. Ashli had always felt her sister's life had been rather restricted. Too narrow.

"Oh, look at the time!'' Helene exclaimed anxiously. "Kyle is picking me up at seven for the dance at the club. I haven't even washed my hair yet!''

"You have more than three hours!'' Ashli observed with dry amusement.

"I despise having to rush. You know that.''

Ashli hesitated. "I've been meaning to ask you something, Helene. Have you and Kyle actually set the date?''

A shadow darkened the other woman's eyes. "Yes, the date has been set. Daddy and Jonas agree that the best time is just before Labor Day.''

"Daddy and Jonas agree? Don't you and Kyle have anything to say about it?"

Helene scoffed. "I've left all the arrangements to Daddy. You know he's so much better at planning things like this than anybody else."

Ashli shook her head in disbelief. "But Labor Day! That's only a month from now!"

Helene put a reassuring arm on her sister's shoulder. "I know what's upsetting you, Ash. You're wondering how on earth you can possibly have your maid of honor gown ready by then!"

"That's not what I'm thinking at all!" she began to protest. "I'm thinking how this is all happening so fast—"

Helene ignored this outburst. "Well, I have a little surprise for you. I ordered your bridesmaid gown weeks ago, in fact. The motif for the ceremony is going to be lavender and dusty rose. All the other girls well wear lavender organza, but because you're the maid of honor, you'll wear the muted pink. I specifically selected it because it will look very flattering with your complexion and hair color..."

Helplessly, Ashli listened as her sister droned on and on about wedding fashions. Didn't Helene realize that clothes were the last thing on her mind right now? She could care less about frilly prom-style dresses at a time like this. Helene was walking into a loveless marriage in a matter of weeks, and she was concerning herself with petty, superficial details!

Mercifully, Helene at last went upstairs to get ready for her dinner date with Kyle. Ashli was left to ponder her own problems. She still had to decide what her plans would be for the fall. She had quietly received her master's degree from the university just this past May. She hadn't wanted to make a great fuss about it, and in fact, had felt somewhat embarrassed even wearing a cap and gown and attending the commencement exercises. It had been a great relief when her father hadn't made the trip out to California after all, to attend the ceremony. But he and Helene had each sent a congratulatory bouquet of yellow roses. Now, the question for Ashli was, what did she intend to do with her degree?

Until last week, she had secretly hoped deep in her heart that Edward DePaul would ask her to collaborate on his new book. She had been convinced that working together in such intimate surroundings as his Los Angeles townhouse would draw them even closer together. Not only would she be working toward her doctorate, but after all these years, perhaps Edward would begin to see her as a woman.

Well, that would never happen now. Ashli's mouth tightened. She shut her eyes and tried not to imagine Edward and Angelique setting up housekeeping in his charming condominium near the university campus. How odd to have devoted herself to a man for five years, only to have a complete stranger arrive out of nowhere and in a matter of seconds, capture the shy professor's heart. No! Ashli stood up from the table abruptly.

It was over, completely over. In fact, it had never even existed. The sooner she stopped thinking about

Edward, the better off she would be. The man was nearly three thousand miles away, and he was lost to her forever. She had to do something to distract herself, to push the miserable feelings away. Well, Ashli smiled bitterly, she could always go for a swim. That had always made her feel better in the past.

Half an hour later, she had changed into a faded red maillot from her high school days. Her body had matured in the past few years. It was still slender, but there were a few more curves, and they were actually flattered by the high-cut legs and deep vee at the neckline of the one-piece suit. It was a relief to plunge into the deep end of the Olympic-size swimming pool, which was set back on a path leading from the side of the house. Even as the sun sank lower in the early-evening sky, Ashli continued to float on one of the inflatable vinyl rafts while alternately swimming a few energetic laps. She did this until she felt both tired and invigorated. The exercise had certainly worked out some of the kinks that her body had suffered during the long drive home. She did one final stretch across the length of the pool, and out of breath at last, made her way to the ladder.

"I have a feeling you need a towel." She heard Kyle Hamilton's familiar deep voice.

"Oh, hi." Ashli hoisted her dripping body out of the water. Even at her full height of five foot six, the man still towered over her.

"Here." With a faint smile, he handed her one of the fleecy, yellow monogrammed pool towels.

"Thanks." Ashli accepted it with an involuntary shiver. She had been swimming for too long, and had lost all track of the time. The cooler air of evening now chilled her soaked skin.

For just a moment, Kyle watched silently as she struggled to grip the towel with her shaking fingers. Then, without a word, he took the towel from Ashli's hands and deftly placed it around her shoulders. The brief touch of his hard fingers caused another involuntary shiver, but this time her reaction had nothing to do with the cold.

"Thanks," she repeated faintly. Strange, Ashli thought to herself. Kyle Hamilton was making her feel the oddest sensation in her stomach. She *really* must have been in the water too long!

The man looked disturbingly masculine tonight, in a lightweight gray summer suit and navy silk tie. "I'm waiting for Helene to finish dressing," he explained.

"So I've surmised," she murmured distractedly, and tried to concentrate on briskly drying her arms and legs.

Kyle made an attempt to look away from her supple, golden-tanned limbs. "Uh, so what was I saying just now?"

Ashli stared at him in astonishment. This was all rather odd. She had never seen the man so ill at ease. "You were saying that you're waiting for my sister to get ready."

"Right," came the hasty reply. "What is it about women?" he asked in a forced, light tone. "It seems to me you all feel it necessary to keep men waiting."

"Do we?"

"Well, it certainly seems that way."

Ashli had to concede that it was definitely a fact of life when it came to Helene. She had never met another human being who fussed so over her appearance. But then again, the results were always so spectacular. She cleared her throat nervously. "In any event, when my sister finally does come downstairs, you'll have to admit that it was well worth the long wait."

For a brief moment, Kyle said nothing. He was watching a single droplet of water as it glistened on the end of one of Ashli's incredibly long eyelashes. As soon as she blinked, the droplet disappeared. "Yes," he agreed vaguely, "Helene always manages to look beautiful."

"You make a spectacular couple."

He crossed his arms. "I suppose that's a compliment."

"Of course. What else would it be?"

"I don't really know. Sometimes I get the distinct impression that you're making fun of me."

She stared at him in surprise. "Why would you say something like that?"

He shrugged matter-of-factly. "Because it's true."

"That's ridiculous."

"Is it?" There was a significant pause. "I told you last night that I had a very good memory."

Ashli flushed bright red beneath her suntan. "Are you saying that you overheard those things I said years ago at the country club?"

"Every word."

"Oh." Right at this moment, she wished she could
have sunk back into the swimming pool. Who would
have ever imagined that Kyle Hamilton had even been
aware of the giggling taunts of a thirteen-year-old girl,
let alone remember what she'd said, after all this time?

Ashli recalled that summer a decade ago. She and
her teenaged girlfriends had watched, totally mystified as their older sisters and all the other vacationing
college coeds had practically thrown themselves at the
reigning Elm Grove Country Club tennis champion.
Who could forget the dashing Kyle Hamilton, recent
Ivy League graduate with his sunbleached hair, winning smile, and powerful physique? On the court and
off, he was always surrounded by a cluster of fawn-
ing, adoring young women—all dazzled by the man
clad in his expensive tennis whites. Oh, sure, Ashli and
her little girlfriends admitted, Kyle Hamilton might
have borne a striking resemblance to one of the most
popular movie stars of the day, but the fact still remained that he was *old*. Twenty-five, at least! That
was practically middle-aged to her and her friends.
Ashli recalled how amusing it had been to watch the
silly behavior of young women whenever they were
near Kyle. The things they would do and say. After a
while, Ashli and her adolescent chums took to mim-
icking them.

"Oh, Kyle!"

"Oh, Kyle!"

"Oh, *Kyle!*"

It became great fun for Ashli and her friends to bat their eyelashes in an exaggerated manner and stand by the edge of the tennis court while Kyle practiced his serve. If he heard their juvenile taunts at all, he never appeared to acknowledge them. But then, the glamourous Kyle Hamilton had always seemed to ignore anyone under the age of eighteen. Perhaps that was the reason Ashli had assumed he simply hadn't noticed the small cluster of twelve- and thirteen-year-old girls, their mouths filled with braces and grape bubble gum as they giggled amongst themselves and recited their favorite cheer:

"Short on substance, long on style—
Kyle, Kyle, with the million-dollar smile!"

They weren't quite sure what the words meant, exactly, but Ashli had penned the little poem after overhearing some of the college boys at the club complaining to one another about the annoying popularity of Kyle Hamilton.

"Puffed-up conceited jerk," she'd overheard one young man mutter irritably. "What do all the girls see in him, anyway? He's all style and no substance."

Now, back in the present, Ashli underwent the scrutiny of Kyle Hamilton's bright blue stare. "Oh, yes," he repeated softly. "I heard every word. You must admit, a man would have to be deaf not to hear the high-pitched chorus of half-a-dozen little girls."

Evidently embarrassed, Ashli started to twist the wet towel between her fingers. "Look, that was all a long time ago. I apologize if it offended you, but we were pretty stupid and tactless little kids."

He shrugged again. "As you say, it was all a long time ago. Forget it."

She smiled sheepishly. "Only if you forget what an obnoxious little girl I was."

Those incredible eyes traveled slowly down the length of her shapely body. "That's no problem, Ashli. You most certainly are *not* a little girl anymore."

She was clearly startled. "Is that supposed to be a compliment?"

"No. It's a fact."

But something in Kyle's tone had already caused goose bumps along Ashli's skin. All at once, she became extremely self-conscious, standing there in her scanty attire. Now that it was wet, the shiny red material of the maillot clung even more tightly to every slender curve of her body. "I . . . I really ought to be going inside now."

He quirked an eyebrow. "Do I make you nervous?"

"Of course not!" she uttered hastily. "It's just that it's time I changed for dinner. Dad hates to be kept waiting."

"Whatever you say."

"This time, I believe you're the one who's making fun of *me,* Kyle Hamilton!"

"No." He reached unexpectedly, and touched a loose, soaked tendril of her brown hair. "The last thing I want to do right now is make fun of you, Ashli.''

It was a startling sensation to feel the warmth of his fingers against her cool, moist skin. Ashli's mouth parted in surprise. "Kyle—" She stared at him in astonishment.

Abruptly, he pulled his hand away. "You're quite right. It's time both of us were going back inside.'' Without another word, he turned on his heels and strode purposefully toward the terrace.

"What in the world—'' Ashli asked his retreating back as she gazed after him in confusion. What on earth had just occurred between them? And why was her heart pounding in her ears? Only yesterday, she had felt so numb that nothing and no one could have had the slightest effect on her. Only yesterday, Edward had been the one person who could cause such an odd flutter in her stomach. But now—

Angrily, Ashli hurled the damp towel onto the concrete. No, absolutely not! Mr. Kyle Hamilton was about to marry her sister. One month from now, he would become Ashli's brother-in-law. She most certainly had *no* interest in him as a man! And if her knees felt just a little weak and shaky right now, it was merely because she still hadn't recovered from the considerable strain of a lengthy and exhausting road trip.

Chapter Three

It had been a long time since Ashli and her father had enjoyed a quiet evening together. It was one of the few things she had missed about Elm Grove.

"Turkey, dressing, mashed potatoes..." Andrew Wilkerson remarked. "Charles, you've certainly outdone yourself tonight."

"I took the liberty of preparing some of Miss Ashli's favorites," the butler said blandly as he poured the wine.

"Thank you for remembering," Ashli said, looking at the butler with affection. How often had she taken his reassuring presence for granted over the years?

"Better watch yourself, Charles," her father observed with a chuckle. "I believe you're becoming more and more sentimental with age."

"Yes, sir," came the cool retort.

After Charles had left the dining room and returned to the kitchen to fetch dessert, Andrew Wilkerson drew a cigar out of his vest pocket and reached for his engraved gold lighter, a precious wedding gift from his late wife. "Ashli, you don't know how happy it makes me to have you home."

She shifted in her chair uneasily. "I'm glad to be back, too."

The older man eyed her knowingly. "Don't you think I can tell by your face how miserable you are? It's all because of that weirdo professor of yours!"

"I don't want to talk about it."

Her father shrugged and bit down on the cigar. "You're my baby and I hate to see you unhappy. For five years, I've stood by while you've mooned over this Edward whatshisname."

Ashli gazed down at the tablecloth blindly. "That's all over. Finished."

"I'm delighted to hear it," he said, nodding approvingly. "Five years is an awfully long time to waste on a blind fool like that. And believe me, sweetheart, any man who isn't head over heels in love with you *is* a blind fool!"

Ashli laughed in spite of herself. "Thanks for that, Dad. You're great for a girl's ego."

"Stick around, dear. I'll do better than that. I'll find you a wonderful fellow, just as I did for your big sister."

"Uh, that's quite all right," she sputtered hastily. "Don't go to any trouble on my account."

"Nonsense," her father declared, waving his cigar expansively. "In fact, I've already got my eye on some wonderful prospects for you, honey. Fine, upstanding young men."

Ashli coughed. "Maybe later, after Helene is married and settled. We'll discuss it then."

Her father beamed. "I'm pleased you've become sensible. I can't tell you how marvelous I feel about the way you two have finally behaved the way daughters of mine should." He leaned over and kissed her cheek. "I thought the happiest moment of my life was last night when Helene and Kyle announced their engagement and made it official. But now that you've come home and left all that lovestruck foolishness behind you, well, what can I say?" He leaned back in the richly upholstered chair and gave a contented sigh. "You've pleased me profoundly."

Ashli was almost embarrassed, but what could she say? It was so touching to see her father in such a euphoric state. "I'm glad," she finally managed to say. This was certainly the wrong time to mention that her stay in Elm Grove was just temporary. How could she tell him right now that her visit home would only be a brief one? All she really needed was some time to get herself together and plan for the future.

Blissfully, Andrew Wilkerson took a deep drag on his cigar. "Yes, sweetheart. This is a happy time for your father. I can admit to you now, that I had doubts that Jonas and I were really going to pull this little engagement off. Oh, I had complete confidence in Helene. She can always be depended upon to do the right thing. The sensible thing. But that young Kyle was always a bit skittish. We had the deuce of a time bringing him up to scratch.''

"That hardly surprises me.'' Ashli couldn't prevent the cynicism from coloring her voice. "Frankly, Dad, I never thought of Kyle Hamilton as the marrying kind.''

"All men are the marrying kind, given the right circumstances.'' He looked at her pensively. "I've noticed how hard you've always been on the boy, Ashli, and I must say I think you judged him somewhat harshly. He's a devoted son to Jonas, and he's the backbone of the family business.''

She quirked an eyebrow. "I find that hard to believe.''

Andrew laughed. "Now, you're still seeing him as that pompous, puffed-up college kid. A man can change, honey.'' He paused. "There are quite a few things about Kyle Hamilton that you know absolutely nothing about.''

Ashli played idly with her napkin. "Such as?''

Surprisingly, her father looked away with an odd expression on his distinguished face. "There are certain matters that I'm really not at liberty to discuss. But just trust me when I tell you that that young man has mettle. He's helped some people out of a few tight spots, believe me.''

"What do you mean by 'tight spots'? What's he done, Dad? Lent a few people some money?'' Ashli shrugged indifferently. "It's not as if he can't spare it. The Hamiltons have even more money than you do.''

"Money has nothing to do with it." He looked at her contemplatively. "I shouldn't really be telling you any of this, but for all his playboy image, Kyle Hamilton has done some pretty courageous things. Life-and-death things."

"I don't understand."

Andrew hesitated. "This is not to be repeated to anyone, Ashli. Do you remember that hostage siege a year ago in that tiny Central American country, Catania?"

She was confused. "Sure I do, Dad. It was all over the television and newspapers for weeks. But what does that have to do with Kyle Hamilton?"

"That's what I'm about to explain. Do you remember that dramatic rescue of those embassy workers by what the newspapers called 'an elite group of professionals'?" Her father shook his head. "That's the official story, honey. But it's not the truth. It's not quite what really happened."

"What are you getting at?"

"That was no 'elite group of professionals' as the news services said. The truth is that the government had virtually given up on all negotiations and was afraid to risk any rescue attempt. The men who went in there and saved people at that embassy were a group of old college buddies. Fraternity brothers, believe it or not."

Ashli blinked. "You're telling me that one of the most dramatic rescues in years was pulled off by—"

"Yes. By a group of aging preppies who wanted to save an old and dear friend. I know it sounds unbelievable. To realize that these were not army commandos. Just a bunch of ordinary men in their midthirties. A lawyer. A doctor. A college professor. A car salesman. I could make a list, but the point is, one of those men was Kyle Hamilton. And he almost didn't make it out of Catania alive.''

Her heart lurched. ''What do you mean, Dad? What do you mean he almost didn't make it?''

''He was shot helping the others through the jungle. The bullet missed his heart by inches.''

She shook her head. ''This is incredible!'' These revelations about Kyle Hamilton were unbelievable, to say the least. Without a doubt, the last thing Ashli had ever expected to hear about the man was that he'd been an honest-to-goodness hero. A man who had risked his life in a remote tropical jungle to save an old friend.

Her father nodded. ''Kyle is lucky to be alive. As it is, it took him almost this entire year to recover from his injuries.''

''I had absolutely no idea.'' For the first time in her life, Ashli was almost at a loss for words.

''So I hope you can understand, dear,'' her father continued, taking another deep drag on his cigar, ''besides the fact that he's the son of my dearest friend, why I'm so proud to have such a courageous fellow as my future son-in-law.''

''I suppose I do,'' she replied. She was dumbstruck and disconcerted. She had totally misjudged Kyle Hamilton. In the past twenty-four hours, her longheld opinion of the country club playboy had under-

gone a radical change. It was still hard to imagine the
always impeccably dressed Kyle with his perfectly
blown-dry blond hair and manicured nails, struggling
through the hazardous jungle underbrush, risking life
and limb. In fact, it was an image almost impossible
to conjure up.

"But remember," her father continued. "You are
not to repeat what I've told you to anyone. It's strictly
off the record."

"But why?"

"Because, my dear. There are certain things that a
man would rather not have generally known. It's a
very private part of Kyle's life."

"What about Helene? She knows, doesn't she?"

Her father shook his head firmly. "No."

"This is ridiculous." Ashli stared back at him in
frustration. She was thinking, if her older sister knew
about her fiancé's heroism, it might increase her ad-
miration and affection for Kyle.

"No," repeated Andrew Wilkerson, "and you must
promise not to say anything about this to Helene. You
know very well what a big mouth she has."

"But still, Dad—"

"But still nothing! Your sister is a beautiful and
charming young woman, but she couldn't keep a secret to save her life. And if the truth behind the Catania rescue operation ever got out, it could spell
disaster for many innocent people."

"Then why did you tell *me*?"

He gave a weary smile. "You're different from Helene in many ways, honey. The least of which is, you can keep a secret."

"That might well be, Dad, but I'm not marrying the man. Helene *is*. Kyle's heroism is something she really ought to know about."

"The reason I told you this in the first place is because I wanted you to understand. I know you've always thought of Kyle Hamilton as... somewhat superficial. It's important to me that you welcome him into our family with the same pride and happiness that I do. It means everything to me to have a son-in-law like Kyle."

It was true, Ashli realized. She had never seen her father looking so downright pleased with himself. It was quite clear that as far as Andrew Wilkerson was concerned, Kyle Hamilton was the son he had always wished for and had never been fortunate enough to have. A part of Ashli felt an ache of jealousy for the void in her father's heart that she could never hope to fill.

It was well before midnight when Kyle's vintage sports car roared into the driveway. Ashli just happened to be lounging in one of the oversize maroon leather chairs in the library. It had been quite pleasant to rediscover some of her favorite books from childhood still stacked in precise, alphabetical order on the fine old built-in oak shelves, which lined the walls of the high-ceilinged room. Tall windows opened up to a balcony, which overlooked the circular en-

trance to the front of the mansion. Curious, Ashli
watched as Kyle walked around to the passenger side
of the sleek classic white Corvette and opened the door
for his fiancée. At that precise moment, he leaned over
and murmured something in Helene's ear. She stepped
out of the car and linked her arm though his.

Suddenly, Ashli felt a tight knot form in the pit of
her stomach. She turned away in haste, and walked
back inside the library, shutting the tall glass doors
behind her. What business did she have, anyway, spy-
ing on her own sister? And why did she feel so strange
watching the two of them together? Perhaps the reason was that everyone seemed to have a man except
her. Perhaps it was the fact that Helene and Kyle made
such an incredibly handsome couple. And her sister
looked especially beautiful tonight, in a short, pink,
silk halter dress, her blond hair swept back in an elegant chignon.

A few minutes later, Ashli heard the gunning of an
engine as Kyle's car disappeared into the night.

"There you are!" Helene leaned against the doorway, and kicked off her leather high-heeled sandals.
"Good grief, you have absolutely *no* idea how much
my feet are killing me!"

"I guess that's what happens when you dance all
evening," Ashli said, feeling strangely envious.

"Hmm, I suppose you're right." Her sister flopped
into another leather chair and continued to flex her
toes. "Kyle is one terrific dancer."

For a moment, Ashli couldn't help but imagine
what it would be like to dance with Kyle Hamilton. To

be held in his arms. For goodness' sake, what was the matter with her? Since when had such traitorous thoughts invaded her mind? Quickly, she cleared her throat. "So, you had a good time tonight?"

Helene gave an indifferent shrug. "Kyle is always an amusing escort." She paused. "I wish he would have said something about my new hairdo." Her manicured fingers patted the sleek chignon. "But I suppose not everyone has an artistic eye."

Ashli stifled a smile. "Like whatshisname, Simon?"

"Who?"

"That young fellow with the shaggy hair. The one who thinks you resemble Queen Nefertiti. The one who thinks you have wonderful bone structure and wants to immortalize you in stone. *That* Simon."

"Oh, him." Helene critically examined her polished fingernails. "I'd completely forgotten about the man."

"Why didn't you ask Kyle to come in?"

Helene arched an eyebrow. "You're certainly Miss Nosy tonight, aren't you?"

"Just asking," Ashli murmured. Actually, she *was* being unusually nosy. Why on earth did she care whether or not Kyle Hamilton came inside the house after his date? Since when did her sister's glittering social life ever concern her one way or the other?

"If you really must know, Kyle didn't ask to come inside and I didn't offer. Frankly, I'm rather exhausted. Everybody at the club was congratulating us on our engagement, and all the men wanted to dance with me. It was rather tiring.'' Helene glanced at her watch casually. "Would you look at the time? It's almost eleven-thirty!"

Ashli was mystified. Since when had her older sister ever complained about the lateness of the hour? If anyone was a night owl, it was most definitely Helene. And tonight was Saturday, no less.

Helene yawned. "Well, I'm totally ragged. I think I'll turn in."

Perplexed, Ashli stared at her. "It's not even midnight."

Her sister gave a thoughtful glance. "Ash, I know you and I haven't had a chance to catch up on all the gossip. I promise we'll have a long chat tomorrow. Okay?"

"Sure." She was totally puzzled now.

"Good night." Helene picked up her sandals by the straps and flung them over her shoulder carelessly.

"Good night," Ashli muttered, as her sister turned and walked from the room. Oh, well. At least she wasn't the only person who was behaving strangely these days.

For another fifteen minutes, she tried to concentrate on the novel she had selected from the bookshelf, but finally gave up. Normally, Ashli had no problem losing herself in a good book. Tonight, however, was a different story. Her mind kept wandering. She couldn't stop thinking about Edward and Angelique. When she tried to force such thoughts from her mind, they were replaced by the equally disturbing

picture of Helene and Kyle standing arm in arm in the
moonlight.

"What's wrong with me, anyway?" she grumbled
aloud. At twenty-three years of age, Ashli felt suddenly old. Just a few weeks ago, she had been a vital,
energetic young woman, happily working side by side
with her colleagues at the dig. With Edward to inspire
her these past five years, Ashli's enthusiasm had been
boundless. Even in the dry, torrid air of the Arizona
desert, she had felt carefree and alive. Life was a joy,
and her heart was filled with a sense of purpose and
accomplishment. All of that was gone now, evaporated in an instant of betrayal.

Oh, Edward hadn't meant to hurt her, and it wasn't
as if she had even told him of the depth of her feelings. But the truth was, a man could always tell when
a woman was attracted to him, couldn't he? And despite his shyness and absentminded nature, could Edward DePaul truly *not* have been aware all these years
of her love for him? Ashli had to confess that it was
unlikely. The painful reality was that he simply hadn't
been attracted to her in the same way she had been to
him.

When the quiet, unassuming Professor DePaul finally fell in love, it had happened for him in an instant. Love did not blossom slowly, after five years of
devotion. Love had arrived like a glorious thunder-
bolt in the shape of Angelique Boulez. With a bitter
sigh, Ashli replaced the leather-bound edition of *Jane
Eyre* on the bookshelf. Love was everywhere, it
seemed. In classic literature. In real life. Everywhere,

wonderful men were falling madly in love with fortunate young women. Why couldn't she have that dizzying effect on a man? Why hadn't anyone ever fallen in love with her? What was wrong with her?

What was the point of sitting around and feeling sorry for herself? Ashli thought. A few minutes later, she made her way upstairs to her bedroom and undressed. She switched off the lamp and quietly stood and watched the glow of the moon through the open window. And that was when she was startled by an unexpected sight. Quite clear in the moonlight, the figure of her sister Helene quickly walked across the back lawn. She was dressed in shorts and a simple T-shirt. Her feet were bare.

"What in the world—" Ashli's words stopped in midsentence, as she saw another tall figure appear on the lawn. A slender young man with shaggy, dark hair. *Simon*. Ashli continued to stare as he pulled Helene into his arms and kissed her passionately. Helene did not seem to be offering any resistance. Instead, she seemed to melt into Simon's embrace.

It embarrassed Ashli to find herself mesmerized by this scene. She felt like a voyeur, but she couldn't pull her eyes away from the hypnotic sight. Just then, Simon drew back from the kiss and began to talk earnestly to Helene. For a moment, they seemed to be arguing about something, but Ashli was too far away to hear any of the words clearly. Finally, her older sister placed a conciliatory hand on the young man's shoulder. The young artist seemed truly angry. He folded his arms across his chest and turned his head away. Helene appeared to be pleading with him. To Ashli, it was all like some dramatic scene being played out in the moonlight. A classic lover's quarrel.

Lovers! Ashli was dumbstruck. Helene and Simon were lovers! Why hadn't she seen it before? The glowing expression in her sister's eyes this afternoon when she'd spoken with the young man. The flush in her cheeks. *Lovers!* And yet, only last evening Helene had proudly announced her engagement to Kyle Hamilton! What in the world was going on here?

Both mesmerized and deeply troubled, Ashli watched silently as the drama on the lawn came to its inevitable conclusion. Simon turned to face Helene again and extended his hand. With a happy laugh, she clasped it in her own and led him away toward the cool shadows of the pool house.

Chapter Four

For the second night in a row, Kyle couldn't fall asleep. With growing irritation, he glanced at the digital clock on the dresser and noted that it was three-thirty in the morning. He reached for a cigarette and leaned back wearily against the headboard. Seldom, in all his thirty-five years, had he suffered insomnia. This new uneasiness was completely alien to Kyle.

By rights, he should have been perfectly content. He was in excellent health. He was one of the most successful real estate developers in the entire state. And he was engaged to marry a woman so beautiful that he was the envy of all his friends. He had fought the idea of marrying Helene Wilkerson for years. Then one day, he finally asked himself what he was waiting for. Some mythical emotion called "love"?

Year after year, he had watched as his male friends fell by the wayside. They either married or plunged into a series of unhappy, ultimately unsatisfying relationships. He had been the best man at half-a-dozen weddings. None of the marriages seemed to last. Kyle's own parents had never been particularly compatible. As a result, he had a rather jaundiced view of the entire institution of marriage. He had supposed that eventually, he would have to marry. A family was something he wanted very much. Perhaps he was getting overly sentimental in his old age, but he wanted a son to carry on the Hamilton name.

But Kyle had no illusions about the kind of wife he would select. She would have to be attractive and well-bred. Love was something that did not even figure into the equation. In fact, emotions would play no part at all in the selection process. The truth was, Kyle had always envied his friends who seemed to fall in and out of love with the frequency of a ham radio. He had never been vulnerable to such neurotic heart flutterings. Come to think of it, over the years, many women had accused him of having no heart at all.

The near-fatal injury he had suffered in the disease-infested jungles of Catania had changed Kyle forever. He took a deep drag of his cigarette. There was nothing like a brush with death to make a man reevaluate his life and consider his mortality. Once back home, on the slow and painful road to recovery, Kyle made the decision to take control of his future. After all those years of pleading and cajoling, Jonas Hamilton was clearly stupefied when his only son finally ac-

ceded to his wishes. Sure, Kyle decided, after taking a
second look at Helene Wilkerson, old Andrew's
daughter had grown up into quite a knockout. And
there was no denying that her manners were impeccable. All in all, the two of them seemed to get along
quite well. Besides, Kyle reasoned logically, he
couldn't ask for a better father-in-law than Andrew.
As a bonus, it certainly pleased his own father more
than anything else Kyle had ever done. So, as far as he
was concerned, marrying Helene was the wise and
sensible thing to do.

He'd thought so until two nights ago, when he'd met
Ashli. She had fallen into his arms at the foot of the
staircase and Kyle's entire logical, well-planned uni-
verse had tumbled down around him.

He remembered the Ashli Wilkerson of ten years
ago as a fat, obnoxious schoolgirl. But all his previ-
ous recollections faded instantly the moment she had
stared back at him with those bewildered hazel eyes.
Holding her against his chest was an unexpectedly delightful sensation. She had the most adorable nose.
Every second longer that he held her in his arms, Kyle
discovered more and more fascinating aspects of
Ashli. The more she talked, the more her voice pleased
him. And that slightly crooked, mischievous smile of
hers was downright captivating. Within twenty seconds of their collision, Kyle became the most miserable man in Elm Grove. Talk about bad timing!

Angrily, Kyle stubbed out the cigarette in the bedside ashtray. If there was such a thing as fate, then this
would have to be its ultimate joke. He had waited all

his life to meet the right woman, and had at last come to the conclusion that there was no such person. It was all a romantic illusion. He had waited all his life to meet the right woman, and then had the incredible bad luck to meet her at his own engagement party. Ten minutes before he and his fiancée were scheduled to announce their engagement. And to add the final, poisoning touch to the ill will of Fate, the right woman turned out to be his own future sister-in-law!

Damn. Kyle had been in many impossible, no-win situations in his life, but nothing had ever made him feel as completely helpless before. Perhaps, if he had met Ashli a month ago, even a week ago...who knows? Sure, she obviously did not think very highly of him. From Andrew's endless eulogizing over the past year, he knew that Ashli was a brilliant graduate student in archaeology. Her romantic preferences obviously ran to the studious, articulate professor-types. But maybe with enough time and persuasiveness, Kyle could have stood a chance of winning her over. At least, he would have given it his best shot. But now, the predicament was completely hopeless. He was already locked in and officially committed to Helene. There was no turning back from the mess he had managed to get himself into. He cursed his own stupidity.

How was he ever going to make it through the wedding ceremony with Ashli standing so near yet permanently out of reach? And in the years to come, how would he ever be able to bear all those Thanksgiving and Christmas dinners with the tormenting presence of his lovely sister-in-law? Eventually, she would marry and bring her own husband to family celebrations and Kyle would not be able to stand it. *That* would be the most difficult part of all. Having to see Ashli with another man...a man who would have the right to make love to her.

Almost shaking, Kyle furiously lit another cigarette. What was the point of torturing himself this way? Hadn't it been enough of a torment earlier that evening to have stood so close to Ashli by the swimming pool? When she'd emerged from the water, looking like an exquisite goddess in that skimpy red bathing suit, he'd felt he would lose his mind. Until that moment, he had almost managed to convince himself that the incident on the stairs had been the product of too much champagne and an overactive imagination. Preengagement jitters, he had almost started to believe. But then, he realized with a lurch of his heart, it hadn't been his imagination at all.

Ashli was lovely and desirable. She was sweet and funny. He had been overpowered by an urge to kiss that tiny droplet of water on her eyelashes. Ashli Wilkerson had always thought he was superficial and not all that bright. He wanted to grab her by the shoulders and exclaim that appearances were often deceptive. He wanted to tell her about the poems he had written in high school that no one had ever read. He wanted to tell her about the rescue mission in Catania where he had almost lost his life. He wanted to convince her that she was all wrong about him. But what was the point?

It was too late. Far too late. Ashli would never know just how close he had come to losing control at the swimming pool. Unable to resist any longer, he had reached out and touched her hair. In another moment, he would have pulled her delectable young body into his arms. For Kyle's own peace of mind, he had forced himself to leave the pool area before making a total idiot of himself.

There was only one solution, he thought bitterly. If he was very lucky, Ashli would go back to the university right after the wedding and he wouldn't be tormented by her presence, day after day. Perhaps his lovely sister-in-law might even decide to pursue her doctorate in California, Hawaii, or even Australia. Then, Kyle wouldn't have to be tortured by the daily reminder of his own stupidity and shortsightedness.

What was it Helene had told him tonight? That Ashli had come back home to lick her wounds after an unhappy love affair. It was then, with excruciating finality, that Kyle had realized that it *was* fate. Ashli Wilkerson would have come home to Elm Grove whether or not there had been an engagement party. Inevitably, the two of them would have met at her home or at the country club. Of course, he would have been instantly entranced. If he had only waited a little while longer before plunging into this idiotic engagement engineered so very cleverly by his own father and Andrew Wilkerson. If he had only waited, he would have been a free man when Ashli had returned to Elm Grove. Free to woo and win her.

Kyle smashed his fist against the padded head-board. It could have been so easy! And surely, with-out having committed himself to Helene, it would have been a completely different story. Both his father and Andrew would have been so pleased at his honorable intentions toward Ashli, that they would have con-spired with him wholeheartedly. One Wilkerson daughter would have been just as good, in the eyes of Jonas and Andrew, as the other. To them, the impor-tant thing was that the families be united. And Kyle would have had to be a blind man not to have realized that it was Ashli who was Andrew's favorite child, not Helene. Yes, it would have all worked out in the end. It could have been so perfectly simple. Instead, it had become a lost dream. The reality was a disaster. He would actually be forced to marry the *wrong* sister.

Never in his life had Kyle felt so terribly trapped as he did now. The worst part was, he knew there wasn't a thing he could do about it. It would take nothing short of a miracle for him to get out of this mess.

And Kyle Hamilton had never believed in miracles.

If Ashli had even the slightest inkling of the tur-moil Kyle was going through, she would have been astounded. He had come over to the house several times during the next few days, and nothing in his cool demeanor had revealed anything out of the ordinary. Just once, when he and his father had joined the fam-ily for a quiet dinner, Ashli couldn't help but notice an almost somber expression on his handsome face.

It was Helene who had been the belle of the evening. All smiles and laughter, she had flattered old Jonas throughout the meal, and teased Kyle about how drastically she intended to redecorate the Hamilton home after they were married. Jonas and Andrew had laughed uproariously, but Kyle had seemed only vaguely amused. He kept motioning for Charles to refill his empty wineglass.

Then, while the coffee was being served, Helene received a phone call and quickly excused herself from the table. Without even being aware of it, Ashli gave her sister a disapproving stare. She wasn't a busybody, certainly, but Helene's bizarre behavior of the past few days had profoundly troubled Ashli.

How could her older sister even stand a chance of happiness with her fiancé, while she carried on a clandestine affair with another man? Of course, it was sometimes considered the "modern thing" to have a last fling before getting married. And of course, Ashli's first loyalty would always be to her sister. Still, she found Helene's conduct disturbing. It unsettled Ashli to be an unwitting party to her sister's secret romance.

She was slowly getting to know Kyle Hamilton, and was beginning to realize that he was a man of substance, after all. She was developing a genuine affection for her future brother-in-law. In fact, if she was completely honest with herself, Ashli was beginning to think about Kyle a great deal.... Oh, that was nonsense! Hastily, she took another sip of wine and evaded Kyle's questioning glance. Every now and then, when he looked in her direction, Ashli found herself feeling unnerved. The *only* reason she was thinking a lot about Kyle Hamilton these days was that the situation with Helene had made her quite uncomfortable. She now saw Kyle as a person, and Ashli hated the thought of *any* person being hurt or betrayed.

It was rather obvious that Kyle had no idea that his fiancée was being unfaithful. Sitting here across the table from him now, and being well aware of her sister's double life, made Ashli feel both awkward and guilty. Well, anyway, she thought with an ironic twist of her lips, at least it all kept her mind off Edward and Angelique.

"So," Kyle said, his deep voice intruding upon her thoughts, "what are your plans for the coming semester?"

"I beg your pardon?" she asked, looking up quickly.

His blue gaze was sharp. "You've been somewhat distracted this evening, Ashli. I suppose your mind must be elsewhere."

"Uh, where else would it be?" Oh, Lord, she prayed in embarrassment. Please don't let the man be a mind reader!

"Where else, indeed?" Kyle paused significantly. "Perhaps your mind is still back in Arizona?"

"Arizona?" Good. He was certainly *not* a mind reader.

Kyle folded his arms and leaned across the table. "Yes, Arizona. I get the distinct impression that your mind isn't the only thing you left behind in the desert.''

"What are you talking about?" Ashli felt strangely cornered. The worst part of it was that Jonas and her father had already left the table and were pouring themselves brandy from the bar on the other side of the cavernous dining room. It was just Ashli and Kyle now, alone at the table.

"Oh, never mind," Kyle muttered suddenly. "It's none of my business, anyway." He reached into the pocket of his linen sports jacket for a pack of cigarettes.

Realizing Kyle knew about Edward, Ashli's hazel eyes widened. "Helene told you." It was a statement, not a question.

The man shrugged as he flicked on his silver lighter. ''What if she did?''

"She had no right..." came the indignant protest.

Kyle eyed her steadily. "Helene is my fiancée. She doesn't keep any secrets from me."

You want to bet? The careless words almost rushed from Ashli's lips, but she bit them back. It was rather humiliating to realize that her own heartbreak was no longer a private matter. She could well imagine, with her sister's propensity for gossip, that every detail of the Edward DePaul debacle was now common knowledge at the Elm Grove Country Club.

"Your silence is deafening," Kyle commented.

"That's because I have nothing to say."

There was a pause. "That professor of yours must have been one incredible guy." There was a hint of sarcasm in his tone.

"I have absolutely no desire to discuss Edward."

"Edward, hmm. So, that's his name." Kyle's mouth twisted. "I assume that he was one of those adventurous intellectual types, just like that archaeologist in the movies. You know, the one with the felt hat, leather jacket, and whip. What was his name again?"

Ashli looked blindly into her empty coffee cup. "Are you doing this on purpose, Kyle Hamilton?"

"Doing what?"

"Trying to make me feel even worse than I do already." She practically glared at him. "Aren't things bad enough without you droning on and on about a subject I obviously have no desire to discuss? Thank you so much for reminding me what a cheerful, upbeat and totally exhilarating summer it's been so far!"

Her outburst clearly astonished Kyle. "I'm sorry," he said in a strangely subdued tone. "I had no idea that I was upsetting you, Ashli."

"Forget it."

"But I don't want to forget it." In truth, Kyle didn't understand what had possessed him just a moment ago. He had never before been intentionally cruel to a woman. It was obvious that Ashli's feelings were still raw and exposed from having been jilted by that egghead professor of hers. He had been well aware of this fact, yet had continued to push and prod.

What exactly had he been trying to prove, anyway? That he was capable of making another person feel almost as miserable as he felt? He looked at Ashli now, with those hazel eyes flashing indignantly. Lord, she was adorable. He had dreaded coming to dinner tonight, knowing how increasingly difficult it was to be in the same room with her.

This evening, Helene was exquisitely dressed in lavender silk and pearls, but even so, there was no way she could compare with her younger sister. In her pastel-pink T-shirt and matching jeans, Ashli seemed as delectable as cotton candy. Not that Kyle had any right to tell her so. When it came to anything pertaining to Ashli Wilkerson, he had no rights at all. Kyle had always been an honorable man. Honorable men did not make passes at their future sisters-in-law. Kyle had always lived by a certain code. It was this code which sent him and his companions into a tiny revolution-torn country to save the life of an old friend.

"Listen," Ashli said, her expression suddenly softening. "I'm sorry. I shouldn't have snapped at you that way. I guess I overreacted."

"Well," he conceded, "the fact is that none of it was any of my business." Kyle hesitated for a moment before speaking. "But as long as we're on the subject, what *are* your plans for next semester?"

Ashli shook her head. "I'm still not sure. I'm sending out some applications to various doctoral programs around the country, but it's really too late for autumn."

"So, what will you do?"

"I'm not sure."

"Have you considered, uh, staying around here?" What on earth was he saying? Kyle wondered dazedly. What were these traitorous words coming out of his mouth? The last thing he needed was for Ashli to remain in Elm Grove any longer than was strictly necessary. The sooner she was out of reach, the far better for his own peace of mind. Now, to his considerable chagrin, Kyle actually heard himself add, "It would mean so much to your father to have you around for a while."

She seemed to consider his words. "Do you really think so?"

"Absolutely. Take my word for it, Ashli. Andrew enjoys having you home very much."

She gazed thoughtfully across the room. It was actually a warm and wonderful feeling to be back home. There was something so secure and comforting about being here amongst the familiar surroundings of her childhood. Ashli experienced a pang of guilt. Why had she stayed away for so long? She instantly regretted all the birthday and holiday celebrations which she had missed over the past several years. Somehow, until a week ago, Elm Grove and her family hadn't seemed all that important. Ashli wondered what could have possibly distorted her sense of priorities. How could she have permitted her blind devotion to Edward and his numerous projects to completely absorb her life for such a long time?

Right now, her father was recounting his latest off-color joke to a grinning Jonas Hamilton. As usual, he told the story with broad gestures, waving his trade-

mark cigar expansively. The two men were quite a
study in contrasts. Andrew was short and wiry, while
Jonas towered above him—broad-shouldered and well
above six foot three.

"Amazing, isn't it?"

Ashli glanced at Kyle. "Excuse me?"

His smile was thoughtful. "Our fathers. Do you
realize that they've been best friends for nearly sixty
years? I wonder what it's like to have a friendship so
deep-rooted and secure that it can withstand the test
of time."

Discussions about lasting friendships gave Ashli a
twinge of envy. Frankly, she didn't have many friends.
Well, that wasn't exactly the truth. She'd always had
a wonderful ability to make friends, but they all
seemed to be the free-spirited types who never stayed
in one place for very long. All she could do to respond to Kyle's observations about friendship was to
murmur blandly, "It must be very nice."

Goodness, it suddenly occurred to her, Kyle Hamilton was looking disturbingly attractive tonight. The
expensive tailored wheat-colored linen jacket and
matching slacks accentuated his deeply bronzed skin.
He had rolled up the sleeves of the jacket to give the
outfit a more casual look, but there was no denying
that Kyle still resembled an ad in a fashion magazine.
Ashli immediately thought of Edward, with his soul-
ful but plain face and perpetually disheveled appearance. Edward had been far from handsome, yet his
appeal had been unquestionable.

Perhaps there was some truth to the observation that women were actually harder on handsome men. Looking back on it, Ashli recalled that the ordinary, unexceptional-looking young men seemed to get more girls than the men who looked like matinee idols. Why on earth was that? Was it because of human nature? Did shy, needy-looking types such as Edward DePaul appeal to women because they seemed so vulnerable? It was a bitter lesson to learn that men like that *weren't* vulnerable, at all. Appearances were so deceptive. She found herself studying Kyle across the table. Strange, Ashli had never noticed how serious those bright blue eyes could look.

"You're staring," he said quietly.

"Am I?" Her face flushed with embarrassment.

"That's quite all right," he responded softly. "Stare all you like. I don't mind." *Not one bit,* Kyle marveled to himself. Did Ashli have any idea what her unconscious scrutiny was doing to him right now?

"Uh, where on earth is Helene, anyway?" she exclaimed nervously.

"She's only been away for a couple of minutes," Kyle commented, seemingly amused.

Ashli felt a tight knot inside her stomach. She wished her father and Jonas would stop chuckling over by the bar and come back to the table. It seemed as if Helene had been gone forever. "Where on earth is Charles with the dessert?" she asked, trying to change the subject.

Kyle quirked an eyebrow. "If I didn't know better, I'd think you found my company rather boring, Ashli."

Hardly. "You might be many things, Kyle Hamilton," she blurted out, "but *boring* is most certainly not one of them."

"I believe that's the first real compliment you've every paid me," he said seriously.

Her green gaze was honest and sincere. "Maybe I'm just starting to realize what an interesting person you truly are, Kyle."

"Do you really mean that?" Kyle asked in a strange voice.

"Of course." At that moment, Ashli became aware of the uncomfortable fact that the two of them had crossed over the line. Somewhere, their conversation had stopped being clever dinner-table repartee and had become something else. Exactly *what* it had become she wasn't quite sure.

"As long as we're handing out compliments," he said slowly, "you look very lovely this evening. You should wear pink more often."

Her fingers on the handle of a china coffee cup actually began to shake. "Thank you." Her tone was calm, but inside, the reality had finally hit her. Kyle was openly flirting. And instead of being shocked, Ashli was enjoying every tantalizing moment of it!

Almost mercifully, Charles's crisp voice shattered the delicious tension. "Would you care for the crème brûlée with raspberry sauce?" He glanced at Kyle. "Sir?"

Kyle tore his eyes away from Ashli. "Did you say something, Charles?"

The middle-aged butler's eyes flickered briefly between the two of them. "Dessert, Miss Ashli?" he paused. "Mr. Hamilton?"

Kyle shook his head, and studied the butler curiously. He *knew*. Despite his carefully controlled tone and bland expression, nothing ever seemed to escape the watchful gaze of Charles Wingate. And in that split second, Kyle had the distinctly uncomfortable sensation that he was being read like a book. But true to his calling, the well-trained servant turned away discreetly and walked with the silver dessert tray toward the other side of the room. But Kyle still felt like a mischievous little boy whose hand had been caught in the cookie jar. He hadn't meant to start flirting with Ashli. Like everything else that had befallen his well-organized life since meeting her that fateful night on the staircase—it had simply *happened*. Despite all his resolve, Kyle just couldn't help himself.

She'd probably been imagining things again, Ashli decided hastily. Men as attractive as Kyle Hamilton had never expressed the slightest interest in her before. Their tastes usually ran to glamourous blondes with great figures. At best, her future brother-in-law was merely being polite. It was perfectly natural for a man with Kyle's country club manners to make flattering remarks to any female as part of the art of dinner conversation. Why read anything else into it? Ashli cleared her throat. "You really should try the crème brûlée. It's Charles's specialty. I'm afraid he'll be somewhat miffed."

Kyle seemed distracted. "I don't mean to hurt the man's feelings. It's just that I don't have much of an appetite this evening."

"Are you ill?"

The hard line of his jaw tensed. "You might say that."

Ashli was concerned. "Don't tell me you've caught that dreadful bug that's been going around this summer. What kind of flu did the doctors call it?"

He lit another cigarette. "Oh, it's not anything like that. I don't have anything contagious, I promise you."

There was an almost imperceptible hint of sarcasm in his tone. She brushed a loose strand of hair out of her eye. "I wasn't worried about your being contagious, Kyle. I only thought—"

"You only thought what?"

"Never mind. I didn't mean to pry."

He shook his head. "You weren't prying, Ashli. I realize you were only being polite. It's obvious that you have a very caring nature."

The gentleness of his unexpected observation completely floored Ashli. It was one of the nicest things any man had ever said to her.

"Don't tell me I've rendered you speechless," Kyle exclaimed.

"Practically." How could Ashli ever explain to him that it was simply taking her a few moments to get over the shock? In the last five minutes, Kyle Hamilton had single-handedly made more flattering comments than she had heard in the past five years. By her own standards, it was a veritable festival of compliments. She had forgotten the wonderful ego boost it was to be on the receiving end of casual male chivalry. Oh, of course, there was nothing serious in it, she reminded herself again. This was all part of Kyle's innate charm. She was convinced her sister's fiancé spoke this glibly to all the women he met.

"So, do you think you might be staying in Elm Grove for a while longer?"

Something in his voice astonished Ashli. She couldn't quite put her finger on what it was. "I...I'm still not sure what I'll be doing." It wasn't just Kyle's voice that struck her. There was also something in his face—an odd kind of tension.

"Sorry about leaving you two sitting here like this." Helene suddenly strode back into the room with a nervous smile on her thin, beautiful face. "You must be bored to death!"

Kyle blew a perfect smoke ring into the air, and continued to gaze toward Ashli. "Actually, Helene, I wasn't bored at all."

"Oh, good," she said distractedly. "So, what's for dessert?"

"Crème brûlée," Ashli spoke up finally. "With raspberry sauce."

"I just love the way Charles makes it," her sister enthused brightly. She placed a well-manicured hand on Kyle's shoulder. "You really should try some, darling."

He smiled tautly. "I don't think so, Helene."

"Well, you're certainly a party pooper tonight!" She followed her comment with a sparkling laugh.

Ashli was puzzled. Beneath Helene's bubbly facade, the strain was starting to show. Obviously, the phone call she had just received had been a source of great anxiety. Ashli could always tell when her sister was trying to conceal something. Worse yet, how long would it take before Kyle finally caught on and realized that his fiancée was keeping a secret from him? Or was it possible—Ashli studied the man across the table silently. Something was obviously disturbing him. There was an odd tension in his entire body. When Helene touched his shoulder possessively the expression in his eyes was one of faint cynicism. Did he already know, she wondered? Did he already sense that there was a new flame in Helene's life?

Oh, people and their endless games, Ashli thought acidly. When would women like her sister stop playing the men in their lives like pieces on a chessboard?

"You might be right," Kyle said, glancing briefly at his gold watch. "In fact, it's time Dad and I were going."

"Why am I not surprised?" Helene said, rolling her eyes. "You've just been no fun at all these past few days, Mr. Kyle Hamilton." She sighed. "Let me guess. You've got to get to sleep early again."

"Actually, yes."

"You're turning into a real old fogy," Helene declared.

"I suppose you're right," Kyle said, nodding quietly. He certainly *felt* old, Kyle added to himself. Just looking at Ashli across the table made him feel a million years old. Just like one of those fossils she studied. No, that wasn't quite true. At least fossils interested Ashli. She was endlessly fascinated with ancient objects. Too bad *he* would never have the chance of arousing her interest the same way. Right now, Helene's proprietary hand on his shoulder made him feel even more trapped and frustrated than he had before.

"Are you teasing my son again?" Jonas Hamilton asked his future daughter-in-law.

"What else is new?" Andrew Wilkerson returned to the table along with his old chum. "Don't be so hard on the boy, Helene. It's the secret to a long and happy marriage."

"Truth of the matter is, Kyle is right," Jonas declared. "We've got a long day ahead of us tomorrow. The investors from San Francisco are flying in first thing in the morning to inspect the lake property."

"Honestly." Helene shook her head in annoyance. "Don't you men ever think about anything except business?"

Andrew frowned. "Really, Helene. You should be very proud of Kyle. He is single-handedly responsible for putting together the entire Shadow Lake deal."

Ashli lifted an eyebrow. "What about Shadow Lake?"

"Shadow Lake," Kyle spoke up finally, "is the jewel in the crown of the whole development plan."

"Development?" There was wariness in Ashli's tone. Since childhood, the small lake nestled in the secluded woods outside of town had been her favorite place to go when she had wanted to be alone. Until colonial times, the area around Elm Grove had been home to several Indian settlements. Ashli had discovered her first arrowhead on the shores of Shadow Lake when she was nine years old.

"You say 'development' as if it were some kind of nasty word," Kyle remarked quietly. "It's not always the case, Ashli."

"Oh?" After five years of observing firsthand the sad remains of once-proud civilizations, Ashli always felt a strange sense of loss for the past, the way things once were. It wasn't just the people who were gone forever. But always, in the name of progress, the old buildings were forever being replaced by the new. Why didn't most people understand how much beauty there could be in the exquisite imperfection of the old? She looked at Kyle now with thinly veiled scorn. "Tell me, please, how developing the lake is going to make it better. I'd be extremely interested to hear your explanation."

Helene giggled, but Kyle's mouth merely tightened. "The property is overgrown and in recent years has managed to earn itself a rather unsavory reputation."

"Unsavory how?"

"Need I spell it out?" He took another drag from his cigarette.

"You know, sweetheart," Andrew said, nodding in agreement with Kyle. "Motorcycle gangs, unruly teenagers—the usual problems that crop up when any place is remote and deserted."

"It broke Kyle's heart to see how run-down and disreputable the area had become," Jonas added. "He's the one who came up with the concept for the Shadow Lake Spa."

"It's the biggest thing that's ever happened to Elm Grove," Kyle asserted firmly. "An exclusive resort complex for the weary executive." He paused. "Not only does it provide a substantial tax base for the town, but the project will create hundreds of new jobs in the area. Jobs that are sorely needed in this economy."

"Oh, don't waste your sales pitch on Ashli," Helene suggested as she took another mouthful of crème brûlée, and giggled again. "If it isn't ancient, dead, or extinct, my dear baby sister doesn't want to hear about it."

"That's not true," Ashli replied coolly. "I'd like to hear more about this project of yours, Kyle."

"Why?" His blue eyes burned into hers. "It's obvious that you don't approve of it."

"I never said I didn't approve—"

"You don't have to *say* anything, Ashli," Kyle retorted frostily. "I can read you like a book."

"I doubt that." She glared back at him. "You're not as all-seeing and all-knowing as you think you are, Mr. Kyle Hamilton."

"Just because I happen to believe that the new can coexist perfectly alongside the old? Just because I'm not rigid and close-minded about the sanctity of the environment?''

"Are you implying that *I'm* rigid and close-minded?" Ashli's hazel eyes narrowed.

Kyle stubbed out his cigarette forcefully in the crystal ashtray. "I'm just saying that there are two sides to every coin, Miss Ashli Wilkerson. It might serve you well to remember that occasionally."

"And what is *that* supposed to mean?"

Kyle shook his head. "How much time have you really spent in Elm Grove during the past five years? When was the last time you took a look around this town and noticed the changes here? When the factory over in Harperville closed down last spring, hundreds of people were left unemployed."

"What's all this now?" Andrew asked, glancing at Kyle, then back at his younger daughter with undisguised curiosity. "Why on earth are the two of you arguing?"

Jonas was grinning from ear to ear. "Don't be a stick in the mud, Andy. I haven't had this much fun in ages. There's nothing like a healthy, spirited argument between a man and a woman to keep things lively. Now I *know* we're all going to be one big happy family!"

"We weren't arguing," Kyle uttered stiffly. "Ashli and I were simply sharing a difference of opinion."

His father's lips twitched. "Son, I haven't seen you this riled in ages." He beamed at Ashli. "Your Dad is right, young lady. Things are never dull when you're around!"

Andrew Wilkerson rubbed his arm absently. "You're right about that. I'm hoping I can find a way to persuade Ashli to stay a while longer this time."

"Forget it," Helene scoffed, slightly annoyed at not being the center of attention. "Ashli never stays around anywhere for too long. She's got to be as free as a bird."

"Sooner or later, even birds want to settle down," Andrew observed, looking at Ashli thoughtfully. "Perhaps a person simply needs a *reason*."

The conversation was extremely embarrassing for Ashli. She felt uncomfortable sitting there while they were discussing her. Unlike Helene, she was not used to being the center of attention. Worst of all, the sudden tension between herself and the usually easygoing Kyle Hamilton was rather discomfiting.

"Dad's already going through that huge computer in his brain," Helene observed shrewdly. "He's making a list of every eligible young man at the country club."

"A pretty and brilliant girl like Ashli shouldn't have a problem at all," Jonas said. Then, he turned to his son. "It wouldn't hurt to help matters along, though, don't you agree?"

"I beg your pardon?" Kyle looked at his father questioningly.

"You know what I mean," he declared. "Kyle has some handsome, successful unattached friends from his college days. Wonderful young men from excellent families."

"Jonas, that's a superb idea!" Andrew practically crowed with delight.

Kyle's jaw tightened. "If that's what Ashli wants, I'd be more than happy to introduce her to several single men."

"Don't trouble yourself," Ashli retorted stiffly.

"Nonsense. It's no trouble at all, if that's what you really want." The words seemed to be jerked from between Kyle's lips.

Ashli was mortified. "It's not what I want at all." How utterly humiliating! Her abysmal social life was now the general topic at the dinner table!

"Don't be an idiot," Helene said, nudging her sister. "I've met some of Kyle's friends and they're positively gorgeous. Let him set you up on a few blind dates."

"No, thanks," she replied coldly. The last thing in the world Ashli wanted or needed was to have Kyle Hamilton set her up with potential mates. It was downright embarrassing that he believed she was so desperate and lonely. Ashli didn't need favors like that from *anybody*.

Andrew gazed at his daughter silently for a moment, and then winked at Jonas Hamilton. "We'll discuss this all later."

Jonas, in turn, gave his friend a conspiratorial nod. "Yes, we can always discuss this at another time."

Kyle gave a cough and glanced down at his watch again. "Speaking of the time, we really ought to be getting home, Dad." His voice was unusually sharp.

"Quite right," agreed Jonas regretfully.

"I had no idea it was so late," Andrew murmured.

Kyle's intense blue gaze flickered briefly in Ashli's direction. Abruptly, he stood up from the massive antique oak dining table. "Believe me, it's later than we all think."

Except for Ashli, everyone else at the table found this statement highly amusing and laughed heartily. The only person in the room, however, who seemed to notice the complete lack of mirth in Kyle's voice was Charles Wingate. Long after the Wilkersons and Hamiltons had left the dining room, the middle-aged butler stood alone with a tray of dessert dishes. A strange, troubled expression shadowed his normally emotionless face.

Chapter Five

Thirty-five years ago, Jonas Hamilton and his good friend, Andrew Wilkerson, tired of having to travel many miles to the nearest golf course, had decided to take matters into their own hands. Together, they founded the Elm Grove Country Club. Located on the site of a former dairy farm, the three hundred acres of rolling land comprised some of the most beautiful scenery in the entire state of Connecticut.

A breathtaking view of the valley below was just one of the pleasures of sitting poolside this afternoon. It had been nearly five years since Ashli had last visited the club. She felt somewhat strange meeting her father for lunch here today. In fact, indolently lounging beneath a candy-striped umbrella, Ashli felt positively decadent. These past five summers, she had be-

come used to working under the bright sun of
California, New Mexico, Arizona, and even Peru. Not
to be laboring at one archaeological site or another
during the summer vacations left Ashli with an empty,
restless feeling.

As the children splashed nearby in the shallow end
of the Olympic-size pool and pretty teenaged girls in
multicolored bikinis giggled over by the snack bar, she
was briefly tormented by thoughts of what she was
missing back in Arizona. Almost every day, the team
unearthed new and exciting artifacts at the pueblo.
Why had she permitted her personal feelings to inter-
fere with the joy of participating in such an important excavation? Oh, who was she kidding, anyway?

So much of Ashli's pleasure in the field of archaeology was connected to Dr. Edward DePaul. She loved
the things *he* loved. She had wanted to become an archaeologist because *he* was an archaeologist. Anything that would draw them closer together was what
Ashli had wanted. Now, sitting here at a poolside table on a balmy August afternoon, she was beginning
to see matters clearly for the first time in years. Was it
possible that she had been so blind, so utterly shallow? Pursuing archaeology as a career simply because she wished to win the heart of her professor? If
this was indeed true, it was a most disturbing thought.

"You shouldn't frown like that. It'll give you wrin-
kles," declared Helene.

Ashli looked up from her tall glass of iced tea. "Oh,
hi." Her sister was looking uncommonly radiant in
crisp white duck shorts and a scallop-sleeved yellow

blouse. Even with her hair pulled back in a tight braid, Helene always managed to communicate an air of elegance.

"Haven't seen very much of you in the past few days," Ashli commented. "By the time you finally come home, I'm fast asleep."

Helene shrugged. "You know how it is, Ash."

"Actually, I don't."

"Kyle loves to stay out late."

"*Does* he?"

Helene narrowed her eyes. "Why, yes. You know what a night owl he is. Just one party after another."

"Imagine that!" Whom exactly did Helene think she was kidding? Ashli knew full well that her sister wasn't staying out late all these nights with Kyle Hamilton.

"Anyway, this is a rare sight." Helene gave one of her sparkly laughs. "My baby sister here at the country club. How many years has it been since you last honored this place with your presence?"

She was definitely trying to change the subject, Ashli thought. "Actually, Sis, I'm having lunch with Dad after he returns from his golf game. I hope you're going to join us." It would be just like old times, she mused longingly. The three of them, all enjoying a delicious seafood salad underneath the huge awning of the club's dining terrace.

"I've already eaten," Helene remarked briefly. "I'm supposed to meet Kyle on the tennis court in a few minutes."

"Oh." Ashli tried to conceal her disappointment, and something else. Was it just a little envy? In the past week, she had begun to experience the strangest sensation whenever Kyle Hamilton arrived on the scene. "Well, have a good game," she said brightly.

Helene seemed uncomfortable and glanced repeatedly at her jeweled wristwatch. "That's what I wanted to talk to you about, Ash. Do you suppose you could do me the teeniest little favor?"

Ashli shrugged. "Sure."

"When Kyle shows up, could you tell him that I had to cancel our tennis date? I've suddenly got a splitting headache."

"Hmm. You've been having a lot of those lately."

"And exactly what is *that* supposed to mean?"

Ashli sighed and set down her glass. "I know this is none of my business, but it seems to me that you've been spending less and less time with Kyle—"

"You're right," Helene said coldly. "It *isn't* any of your business."

Ashli was growing increasingly frustrated with this conversation. "You're getting married in less than three weeks. How in all good conscience can you be carrying on an affair with another man?" There. She had said it at last.

"W-what are you talking about?" Helene stammered.

"Give me a break," Ashli retorted. "I know all about what's been going on with you and Simon."

Her sister's face was pale. "It's not what you think," she exclaimed hastily. "Simon and I are just . . . good friends. I can *talk* to him."

Ashli rolled her eyes. "Oh, please."

"There's no affair," Helene insisted nervously. "Simon is an artist, remember? I told you he wanted me to pose for him and that's *all* I'm doing. It's perfectly innocent."

"At one o'clock in the morning?"

Helene froze. "What do you know about that?"

"You've forgotten about the wonderful view from my bedroom window, sister dear."

There was a long silence. Then finally, Helene asked worriedly, "Are you going to tell anyone?"

"Of course not," Ashli answered gently. "My first loyalty is to my big sister, you know that. The point is, how fair are you being to Kyle?"

"What Kyle doesn't know won't hurt him."

"How can you say that? The man is going to be your husband! What about his feelings?"

Helene arched an eyebrow. "You seem rather overly concerned with Kyle and his so-called feelings all of a sudden."

Ashli lowered her eyes evasively. "It's just that I'm beginning to realize what a decent person he is. I don't think it's fair to deceive a man like that."

Her sister pursed her lips. "Well, Ashli, if you are so interested in Kyle, perhaps *you* ought to be the one to marry him!"

She practically choked on her iced tea. "What?"

"Oh, that's right," Helene scoffed. "You wouldn't consider marrying anyone. You've got to be as free as a bird."

"Helene!" Ashli exclaimed, truly shocked. "How can you speak so cavalierly about this? Don't you have any feelings at all for Kyle?"

"Sure, I do. He's handsome and we have a great deal in common."

"Is that all you can say?"

"What else do you want me to say?" Helene muttered irritably. "For heaven's sake, you act as if marrying the man was *my* idea!"

Ashli was aghast. "Are you telling me that you really don't want to marry Kyle?"

Helene bit her lip. "I told Dad that I would. And we threw that huge party. Do you realize how stupid I would look in front of all my friends if I backed out now?"

This entire situation was absurd, Ashli marveled. Absolutely absurd. "Helene, I don't understand what the problem is. If you really don't want to go through with the wedding, then who cares what Dad and all your so-called friends think?"

"*I* care." Helene leaned across the table and drank a few sips of Ashli's iced tea. "What other people think has never been important to you. I mean, your entire life, Ash, you've always done things to please yourself. When was the last time you did something because it was what Dad wanted you to do?"

"Really, Helene. I realize that other people's opinions have always mattered a lot to you," she said dryly. "Personally, I can't quite figure out what you see in all these snooty friends of yours. As far as Dad goes, though, it's one thing to want to please him, but allowing him to select your husband is going just a little bit too far. How hard could it possibly be to say *no* to Dad just once in your life?"

Helene slammed the glass back down on the enameled table. "Oh, it's so easy for you! So very easy! You've never had a sense of family responsibility. Well, it so happens that *I* do!"

"Your only responsibility should be to yourself." Ashli shook her head firmly.

"I don't want to argue about this anymore." Helene perched her red designer sunglasses back onto her nose. "Besides, you'll be gone in a few weeks, anyway. It's not as if you ever stay around long enough to be particularly interested in what's important to Dad. No, that's something which is always left to me."

"Helene," Ashli said slowly, "do you resent me that much?"

"Yes, I do," her sister admitted frankly. "Would you rather I candy-coated it and lied?"

"No." This was a side of her sister that Ashli had seldom seen. She had never been aware of the full extent of Helene's bitterness.

"Oh, don't look so offended. I'm sure all sisters harbor some deep-rooted hostilities toward each other. It's perfectly natural. I've read about it in all the women's magazines. Besides—" Helene said, offering a faint smile, "as long as we're being so honest with each other, isn't it about time you confessed that you've always been more than just a little resentful of *me?*''

Ashli stared back in astonishment. "What on earth are you talking about?"

"Oh, please. Do I have to spell it out? You've always been jealous of the way I look."

"I have not!"

Helene crossed her arms knowingly. "*Now* who isn't being honest?"

Well, Ashli was forced to admit, it had never exactly been a sheer delight growing up in the shadow of such a beautiful sister. But she hadn't been resentful, either. No matter what Helene chose to believe. "I've never resented you," she protested softly. "And that's the truth."

"Fine, whatever you say." Her sister looked at her watch again. "Look, let's not argue about this anymore. If your sisterly loyalty is as sincere as you claim, then do me this small favor and make my excuses to Kyle." She put a conciliatory hand on Ashli's shoulder. "Please, Ash. I really need you to do this for me."

Ashli sighed heavily. "Why are you putting me in this position? You know how much I hate having to lie to anybody."

"When was the last time I ever asked you to do something for me?" It was hard to ignore the pleading in her tone. "Ash, just this once. Please."

Her glamourous sister seemed so vulnerable and unhappy. Ashli knew she was going to give in to her request. "All right," she conceded. "I'll make some excuse to Kyle."

Helene beamed. "Thanks, you're a doll." She bent over impulsively and bestowed a rare sisterly peck on Ashli's cheek. "I really appreciate it."

"Yeah, I'm sure," Ashli muttered ruefully as she watched her older sister walk away from the pool area with a lilt to her step. It didn't take a brain surgeon to figure out where Helene was going. Obviously, she was on her way to a secret afternoon rendezvous with Simon, the raggedy artist. Didn't she realize that she was skating on perilously thin ice? Kyle Hamilton did not impress Ashli as the kind of man who would tolerate being one side of a romantic triangle.

Why couldn't Helene just come out and tell Kyle she wouldn't be able to play tennis with him? Ashli grumbled to herself now, as she made her way down the path to the tennis courts. Even before rounding the other side of the clubhouse, she could hear the fast, hollow rhythm of the numerous volleys. For years, she had envied the people who were gifted with the ability to be brisk, efficient tennis players. The truth was, mastering the game had always eluded Ashli. Not only did she lack Helene's icy, blond beauty, but she also lacked her sister's athletic skill.

She thrust her hands into the pockets of her faded denim shorts and walked gingerly down the rest of the uneven stone pathway. In the distance, she could see Kyle leaning against one of the towering elm trees, chatting with a circle of friends. Even at this distance, there was no denying how attractive he looked. Almost an identical but older version of the way he had looked ten years ago. His bronzed skin so dark against the white of his shirt and shorts. The aviator sunglasses. The straight, blond hair was clipped much shorter than he used to wear it, and there were new lines of weariness around his eyes and mouth. Other than that, not much else had changed.

As his head turned in her direction, and he watched her approach, Kyle's expression behind the dark sunglasses was unreadable.

"Hi, Ashli!" several of the men called out amiably. They were all men in their late fifties and early sixties—men who had been members of the club since it had been founded. All friends of her father, they represented the cream of Elm Grove society.

"I can't believe how grown-up you are!" declared Buddy Windsor, with a huge grin on his red, jovial face. He was the town dentist.

"Makes me feel older than the hills," murmured Joe Haskin, the owner of Haskin's Ice Cream Parlor. Ashli remembered him as being one of the few men in Elm Grove who had always sported a beard.

Somebody motioned in their direction just then, and Myron Weiss, the editor-in-chief of the *Elm Grove Gazette* picked up his racket. "I'd like to inform all of you old fogies that our court is now ready." He turned to Ashli cheerfully. "It's good to see you back, honey. Next time, don't stay away so long. Your dad really misses you."

"All right, all right," boomed Yancy Brown, the bespectacled local attorney and Myron's doubles partner. "Do you want to stand around and flirt with all the pretty young girls, or do you want to play tennis?''

"Now that's a dumb question, Yancy," guffawed Joe with a mischievous wink at Ashli. "Who cares about tennis?"

All the men laughed at this, except Kyle. He just stood there silently, with his aluminum racket slung over his shoulder, and watched Ashli. Moments later, the foursome departed noisily for their court, and Ashli and Kyle stood alone on the grass.

"Why do I get the impression, unlikely as it may seem, that you're here to see me?" he finally inquired.

"I am." Ashli was unprepared for the spontaneous smile that suddenly lit up Kyle's hard features.

"Let me guess. After all these years, you've suddenly been seized by an uncontrollable urge to learn how to play tennis."

"Not exactly."

Kyle didn't appear to hear her. Instead, he continued to smile winningly. "Forget about lessons from the club pro. You couldn't ask for a better instructor than me, Ashli." Unable to resist showing off, he started balancing the racket skillfully on the tip of his index finger. "I hate to brag, but need I remind you that I've been the Elm Grove singles champion for ten of the past sixteen years?"

"Listen, Kyle," she began awkwardly.

"I know, I know," he grinned. "You don't have a racket. That's no problem. Although," he paused, "the dress code is still rather strict. They probably won't let you on the court in that outfit, as attractive as it is." And it was bewitchingly attractive, Kyle thought to himself with an inward groan. Those cute little blue shorts and that skimpy white halter top. Her clothing revealed almost as much of Ashli's tanned and shapely body as that delicious red swimsuit she had worn that evening by the pool. That was an image Kyle still found impossible to remove from his mind. Seeing Ashli looking so sexy again today, well, no doubt about it—getting a good night's sleep was becoming more and more difficult.

"Kyle," she repeated insistently, "I'm here because Helene wanted me to tell you she's had to cancel your tennis date." Lord, she hated lying to people, especially to Kyle Hamilton. Dishonesty was a trait Ashli found particularly distasteful.

"Oh," Kyle remarked quietly. Strange, during the past few minutes, he'd forgotten all about Helene. But then, that always seemed to happen whenever her adorable little sister came on the scene.

He looked so tense all of a sudden, Ashli thought warily. Obviously, Helene's abrupt cancellation must have been a great disappointment. "I'm sorry," she said softly.

He studied her face for a moment. "Are you?"

"Of course."

"What exactly is wrong with Helene, anyway?"

"W-well," Ashli stammered, "she had a dreadful headache and went home."

"I see." There was a grim silence. "A headache."

How terribly awkward this was. Ashli hated every moment of having to lie to him. "Yes."

"It seems to me that my fiancée has had quite a few headaches this past week."

She cleared her throat quickly. "In any event, Helene asked me to convey her regrets."

He twisted his lips in faint cynicism. "Her regrets? Is that what she really said, Ashli? Or are you putting words in your sister's mouth?"

An embarrassed flush warmed her cheeks. "I'm not doing anything, Kyle, except delivering the message that Helene asked me to. I've done it, and now, I'll leave." Nervously, she brushed a loose strand of brown hair away from her forehead. "Sorry about your tennis game."

He pulled off his dark glasses and frowned. "What's your hurry, Ashli? Catching a train?"

His change of tone caught her completely off guard. "No. I'm meeting Dad for lunch."

"Oh, I see." Kyle's intense blue stare was rather unsettling. "I guess you have no time to stop and chat then."

She glanced at him in surprise. "Not really. Dad's probably finished with his golf game by now, and waiting for me in the clubhouse." Ashli looked down at her wristwatch hastily. "Yes, I'm sure he's sitting in the lounge and is probably quite impatient by now. You know how Dad hates to be kept waiting."

"It seems to me," Kyle said, crossing his arms, "that we've had this conversation before."

"Have we?"

The crinkles around the corners of his eyes deepened. "I see that I still make you nervous, Ashli."

She swallowed. "That's ridiculous."

"Hmm. Whatever you say."

Did he have to keep staring at her in that extremely disturbing way? Ashli wondered, ill at ease. And why in the world was she finding it so difficult to look away from Kyle's tanned, muscular forearms? It was fascinating the way those golden hairs stood out against the roughened, bronzed skin. As a teenager, Ashli could remember the sheer strength of those arms. Kyle Hamilton's famous power serve had been the talk of three counties. Ten years later, the man was still in superb physical condition, with not an ounce of flab visible on his body....

Wait a minute! What was she going on about now? Ashli was scandalized. Was she forgetting again that these were not the kind of thoughts a woman should be having about her future brother-in-law? Once again, Ashli found her mind straying in the most dangerous directions. She was forced to remind herself, yet again, that in the matter of Kyle Hamilton, such thoughts were strictly off-limits. Forbidden.

"Is something wrong?" Kyle's deep voice intruded on her troubled thoughts.

"No, nothing!" she almost shouted.

"A rather convincing reply," Kyle observed mildly. "Anyway, since I've been stood up on my tennis date, would you mind if I joined you and Andrew for lunch?"

Ashli raised her eyebrows. "Why do you want to have lunch with us?"

He shrugged. "Because I'm *hungry*."

"Oh."

"Besides, how can you possibly object? I'm practically a member of the family."

What was she supposed to say? Ashli thought uncomfortably. Short of being rude and ungracious, there was no way to turn down such a reasonable request. Just because she felt so terribly awkward in the man's presence, was no reason to avoid him as if she were a frightened rabbit. The sooner she got used to being around her sister's future husband, the easier it would be. Ashli tried to sound as casual as possible. "Of course, you're welcome to join us. I'm sure Dad will be delighted." The truth was, her father enjoyed the company of Kyle Hamilton immensely.

"Why do I get the impression that *you're* less than thrilled?" he asked dryly.

"I hate to disillusion you, Mr. Hamilton, but I'm not concerned one way or the other."

Kyle's expression became unreadable. "No, I suppose not." It had been foolish of him to believe that Ashli might care just a little. What a completely humbling effect she was having upon his inflated ego.

The conversation between the two of them was stilted and brief as they made their way back up the path toward the clubhouse. When she and Kyle entered the main lounge, there seemed to be an unusual degree of activity. Several of the members stood in tight groups, speaking in low, hushed voices. Everyone, including the waiters and the rest of the club staff fell suddenly silent the moment Ashli came into the room.

"I wonder what's going on?" Kyle murmured, curious.

Instinctively, Ashli felt a tug on her stomach. "Something is wrong."

"Don't jump to any conclusions," Kyle remarked in a calm tone. "Wait here a minute, Ashli. I'll be right back."

She nodded, unsure of herself, and watched as he quickly walked toward the staff director. She could see Kyle's entire body stiffen as the other man spoke to him urgently. Moments later, Kyle was back at Ashli's side, a solemn expression on his face.

"What is it?" she asked warily. "Tell me what's wrong."

Without hesitating, he reached for her hand in a reassuring gesture, and walked her back toward the exit. "Listen to me, Ashli," Kyle began calmly, "I don't want you to get upset—"

"It's Dad, isn't it?" Her hand tightened on his. "What's happened to Dad?"

"He had a heart attack out on the golf course."

"Oh, God!" Ashli was horrified. "Is he—"

"No." Kyle stilled her gently with both hands on her shoulders. "He's still alive. Right now, he's on his way to the hospital."

She was sick with fear and worry. "I've got to get there, Kyle!" Blindly, she tried to remember where her car was parked. Where were her car keys? Why did her arms and legs suddenly feel so numb?

"Come on, honey." Kyle firmly led her outside. "I'll drive you to the hospital."

Without protest, Ashli allowed herself to be guided to the parking area. She had no recollection of being helped into the passenger seat of Kyle's white convertible, or of the gentle hands that securely fastened her safety belt. Even the long drive to the county hospital was a blur. But the one thing that Ashli would always remember was how Kyle had stayed with her through the entire ordeal. During the next few tense hours in the hospital waiting room, he never left her side. Jonas Hamilton was there, as well, his hawklike features ashen and strained.

"It's going to be all right." Kyle kept his hand tightly clasped around Ashli's. "I just know everything is going to be fine."

"How can you be so sure?" she responded dully. "Why haven't we heard anything yet?"

"Listen to me," he said, cupping her chin tenderly in his hand. "Andrew is tough. He's going to pull through this."

After what seemed like an eternity, Dr. Montrose came into the room. A kindly man in his late fifties, he gave Ashli a solemn smile. "Your father is a lucky man, Miss Wilkerson. He's suffered a mild heart attack, but he's going to be all right for now."

"What do you mean, for now?"

"This incident was a danger signal, a warning more than anything else."

Ashli bit her lip. "Could you just tell me what that means?"

"Your father is not a young man, and he's been putting too much strain on his heart. He works too hard, he smokes those damn cigars—" There was a significant pause. "And he has absolutely no business playing eighteen holes of golf on a hot day like this."

"But if he stops doing all those things," Ashli interjected optimistically, "everything will be fine again?"

"Don't misunderstand," Dr. Montrose said, shaking his head. "Your father has sustained damage to his heart muscle. We won't know the extent of it for several months. Even with a significant change of life-style, he's never going to be the same as he was."

"What are you trying to tell us?" Jonas demanded.

"In any other case, I might have recommended surgery, but at his age, an operation is too risky." He placed a reassuring hand on Ashli's shoulder. "I don't want you to worry. But for now, your father is going to have to take things easy. No stress, no strain, and most of all, no surprises."

Ashli drew in her breath. "I understand."

"Good." The doctor gave a brisk nod. "You can go in and see him now, but just for a moment."

After Ashli left the room, Jonas glanced at his son. "Where on earth is Helene?"

"I don't know."

"What do you mean, you don't know? She should be here."

Kyle's mouth tightened. "Yes, she should be."

"Well?"

"We couldn't reach her."

Jonas quirked a bushy gray eyebrow. "You couldn't reach her? Didn't you try the house?"

"She's not there. I spoke to the butler."

"Where the hell *is* she, then?"

Kyle gazed down at the linoleum floor. "I haven't the faintest idea."

His father stared at him in puzzlement. "I'd call that rather strange."

"I'd call it something else," Kyle retorted cynically.

"What on earth are you implying?"

Kyle sighed. "Dad, I've put this off long enough. It's time you and I had a little talk."

From his hospital bed, Andrew Wilkerson smiled weakly at his daughter. "I guess your old man isn't as spry as he thought he was."

"Don't try to speak, Pop," Ashli gingerly touched his forehead. It was upsetting to see him like this—so pale and vulnerable, with tubes in his arm. Never in her life could she remember her father ever being ill. He had always seemed the picture of robust health and vitality.

"Don't stop me from talking," he grumbled faintly. "If I don't talk now, when the heck am I going to?"

"Dr. Montrose says we can take you home in a few days."

"The hell with doctors," Andrew murmured. "Listen, sweetheart. This is important." He seemed truly distressed. "We can't let this . . . stop the wedding."

"Forget about the wedding for now."

"I can't forget about it," he insisted, his breathing labored and heavy. "I can't let everything fall apart."

"It won't, I promise you." At this moment, Ashli would have said anything to prevent her father from getting any more upset than he was already.

He closed his eyes. "You don't understand, Ashli. Things have a way of falling apart when I'm not around."

She shook her head quickly. "Don't worry. Nothing is going to go wrong."

Andrew looked alarmed. "Where's your sister? Where's Helene?"

Ashli smiled at him reassuringly. "She'll be here later, Pop." Where on earth *was* Helene? she wondered angrily.

Her father shut his eyes. "Can't let anything stop the wedding, Ashli. I've waited so long for this . . ." His voice started to trail off. "Don't let anything happen . . . Please don't let anything go wrong . . ."

Andrew drifted off to sleep. For a long time afterward, Ashli stood at his bedside in grim silence and gazed at her father's troubled face.

Chapter Six

Helene finally turned up later that evening, remorseful, her eyes brimming with tears. "Why didn't you call me?" she whispered harshly to Ashli.

"Where was I supposed to call you?" her sister retorted in a frustrated tone.

Helene didn't have an answer for her. She simply burst into a fresh bout of tears. And for the next few days, her eyes were red-rimmed and swollen. For the first time in her life, the usually impeccable blonde didn't seem to care about her personal appearance. Neither did it seem to perturb her that Jonas Hamilton now regarded her with a thinly veiled expression of disapproval. Furthermore, the fact that Kyle seemed even more aloof than ever did not appear to concern Helene in the slightest. It was almost as if she were emotionally isolated from everyone around her. Helene even found it difficult to visit her father for very long. "I have this *thing* about hospitals," she explained uncomfortably.

"Then get over it," Ashli said, wanting to shake her. "Dad needs to know we're with him."

"All he ever does is ask about the wedding. Well, I don't want to *hear* about this stupid wedding anymore!"

"Helene!" Ashli's own voice was barely above a hush. "If he wants to talk about the wedding, let him. You remember what Dr. Montrose told us."

"I know, I know," her sister replied irritably. "No arguments. No stresses. No surprises."

"My sweet little girls," Andrew Wilkerson murmured weakly from his hospital bed, as he awoke from another nap. "The only thing that's kept me going is the comfort of knowing that one of you is getting married."

"Yes, Daddy," Helene said, her smile a tight line across her impassive face.

Their father gave a satisfied sigh and sank back peacefully against the pillows. "You've made me the happiest man in the world, Helene. Jonas gains a wonderful daughter and I gain a delightful son. The joining of our two families has been a lifelong dream."

"Yes, Daddy," Helene repeated in a thin voice.

Later, in the hospital corridor, she was not as docile. "Why is Dad pressuring me this way?"

Ashli folded her arms across her chest. "You didn't seem to think he was pressuring you before. Why the sudden change in attitude?"

"I tell you, he's pressuring me!" Helene practically shouted.

Ashli blinked. "The wedding means a great deal to him. You know that."

"Well, *you* might as well know." Then Helene paused significantly. "Last night Simon asked me to marry him."

"What?"

"Oh, I know what you're going to say, Ash. You're going to say 'I told you so!'"

"No, I'm not."

Helene ran a nervous hand through her long, blond hair. "Simon loves me. And I love him."

"I see."

"No, you *don't* see. I was perfectly content until a few days ago. I was going to marry Kyle and live in that wonderful Hamilton mansion." She threw her arms up in the air. "How can I do that now? Simon won't share me with another man. He says I have to choose."

Ashli was torn. She wanted her sister to follow her heart, but this was hardly the right time. The slightest upset to their father could be disastrous. "I don't know what to say, Helene."

"You don't have to say anything," she exclaimed tearfully. "I won't have Daddy or Jonas or anybody else try to put me through a guilt trip. I can't lose Simon. I *won't* lose him!"

"Okay, now wait a minute," Ashli began calmly.

"I can't wait, don't you understand that? Simon is leaving for Vermont tomorrow. Before Daddy got sick, I had agreed to go with him."

Ashli stared at her sister, flabbergasted. "Are you serious? You've only known the man a week at the very most!"

"That's not important," she sniffed. "Simon says if I really care about him, I'll still come. He says Daddy has manipulated me all my life, and tried to mold me in his image."

"Your friend certainly has a lot to say for himself," Ashli muttered critically.

Helene pursed her lips. "I happen to believe that he's right. I've spent my whole life doing exactly what Daddy wanted, always trying to please him, never thinking about what *I* wanted to do." Her eyes narrowed. "Not that trying to please him mattered. Even when you were thousands of miles away, you were still his favorite. You never had to do *anything!*"

Oh, not this old argument again, Ashli groaned inwardly. "Listen, Helene," she declared. "I'm not saying you shouldn't marry Simon, if marrying him is what you really want. I just think you shouldn't rush into it."

"No," Helene asserted, tossing her blond hair defiantly. "I know very well what you're thinking. You want me to wait until Daddy comes home, and then you'll both be able to talk me out of it."

"That's baloney."

"And it would probably work, too," Helene continued. "Daddy has always been able to talk me out of anything. I'm just not as strong-willed and independent as you, Ash. But this time, it's going to be different. I'm not going to wait until Daddy comes home from the hospital and manages to change my mind!" Without waiting for a response to her unexpected outburst, Helene turned and fled down the corridor.

Ashli simply stood there, a stunned expression on her face. In the space of only a few days, love had completely changed the face of her older sister. Just as it had been for Ashli with Edward, Helene's love for Simon had been completely unexpected. Certainly, if marrying Simon made Helene happy, Ashli was all for it. In the meantime, there was still a very big problem. "How on earth will we ever explain this to Dad?" she wondered aloud ruefully.

"Probably the same way I explained it to *my* father," answered a deep voice behind her.

Startled, she whirled around to see Kyle emerge from around the corner. "How long have you been hiding there?"

"I wasn't hiding." There was a strange look on his face. "I was on my way to talk to Helene. I could hear your voices all the way down the hall."

Ashli's hazel eyes widened. "How much did you hear?"

Kyle twisted his mouth. "Enough to know I've just been jilted."

"I'm sorry."

He gave her a vague smile. "I'll get over it."

She glanced at him sharply. "You don't seem very upset."

"Actually, I'm rather relieved."

"You're *what?*"

"You heard me, Ashli. I said I'm relieved."

An odd sensation fluttered through her stomach. "Well, excuse me if I'm a little shocked. For two people who were about to get married, neither you nor my sister seem to have much of an emotional investment in each other."

"I suppose not," he admitted.

Ashli shook her head in disbelief. She would never understand people like Kyle and Helene. She would never understand what motivated their strange behavior. And then, she recalled what Kyle had said moments ago. "Wait a minute. What did you mean before, about explaining something to your father?"

Kyle crossed his arms and leaned against the wall with a deliberately casual air. "If you must know, I merely informed him that I'd reconsidered my engagement to Helene, and decided that there was no way I could go through with it, after all." There was a hint of a twinkle in his bright blue eyes. "As coincidence would have it, your sister actually beat me to the punch, to quote an old cliché."

Her throat felt suddenly dry. "What changed your mind?"

Those incredible eyes flickered over Ashli's body. "A number of things."

"I don't understand."

Kyle hesitated. "Let's just say I finally realized how ill-suited Helene and I are to each other."

"I see."

No, Kyle thought in mild frustration, Ashli didn't see at all. Until a few moments ago, he had never believed in miracles. But now, after having blundered into the hospital corridor and overheard Helene's startling confession, Kyle wanted to do handsprings down the hallway. He felt like a man who had just been rescued from the brink of disaster. Good heavens, he wanted to meet this Simon fellow and personally shake his hand. That's how grateful he was. Kyle tried to stifle his elation. No, Ashli would never understand.

Never before had he ever known a young woman so totally unaware of her allure. He had to suppress the urge to reach out and touch Ashli's glossy brown hair, and tell her how much she meant to him. Even though Kyle felt as if a tremendous weight had just been lifted from his shoulders, and even though his heart was bubbling over with a strange kind of recklessness, he knew he had to control himself. This was not the time to carelessly blurt out his feelings. *You're the one who changed my mind,* he wanted to shout. *You're the woman I want!*

Standing alone in the corridor with her like this, all sorts of wild fantasies rushed through Kyle's normally calm mind. Now that he was a free man, the range of possibilities were endless, but what was the best way to approach Ashli? He couldn't very well just pull her into his arms, kiss the breath out of her, and suggest they elope that afternoon, could he? No, of course not. He would have to handle Ashli cautiously and slowly, so as not to scare her away. Suddenly self-conscious, he cleared his throat and remarked, "You realize, of course, that there's nothing you can do about this situation right now. Your Dad is resting, and we can all deal with it when he comes home tomorrow."

Ashli nodded. "Yes, you're right."

"Until then, there really isn't anything to be gained in worrying yourself." Kyle's mind was racing a mile a minute. "My suggestion is that we both take our minds off what's happened."

"That's easier said than done."

"Oh, I don't know," he murmured. "Right now, I could use a good stiff drink. How about you?"

Ashli felt the strange fluttering sensation in her stomach again. "A drink?"

"It's sort of traditional," Kyle said, attempting to look woebegone. "A jilted bridegroom always goes out and gets himself a drink or two." There was a pause. "And I could really use the company. How about it, Ashli?"

She hesitated. For the first time since her return to Elm Grove, Kyle Hamilton was no longer the property of her beautiful older sister. And now, in a bizarre turn of events, the man was actually asking her out for drinks. He was no longer Helene's future husband. Now, at this moment he was just a man—a most disturbingly attractive man. "I don't know if that's such a good idea."

He raised an eyebrow. "Why not? After the past few days, I dare say you could use a drink, yourself."

No doubt about that, Ashli thought. But aloud, she found herself stammering, "I—I probably shouldn't."

Kyle glanced at her sharply. "Do you think I have some ulterior motive?"

"No, of course not!" She was embarrassed. "It's just—"

"It's just that you're concerned about how it might look," he finished dryly. "The ex-fiancé of Helene Wilkerson seen in a bar with her own baby sister?"

"That's not true," she protested. "I couldn't care less what other people think."

"Oh, is that so?"

Ashli crossed her arms assertively. "Yes."

He nodded with satisfaction. "Good, then you'll come."

"I—" Whatever further protestations she was about to offer died on her lips. She wanted to accept Kyle's invitation. Why deny it? Besides, Ashli chided herself, what was she making such a fuss about? She'd simply join the man for a sociable drink and then go straight home. As Kyle had said, it had been a difficult week for each of them. They could use the company right now. Since when was there any harm in that?

The Black Swan was an unpretentious restaurant and cocktail lounge located five miles outside of town. On the outside, it was an undistinguished one-story brick building. The interior had remained unchanged since the early sixties. There were a dozen or so tables with matching captain's chairs for patrons brave enough to try the dinner menu. But the most appealing aspect of the Black Swan was its dimly lit bar area with a huge tropical fish tank built into the wall.

It was scarcely four o'clock in the afternoon when Kyle's sports car pulled up alongside Ashli's pickup truck in the gravel parking strip. Except for the bartender and an elderly couple playing at the pinball machine, the place was deserted.

"I doubt we'll run into anybody we know," Kyle observed wryly, as he escorted her to a small table in the corner.

"I already told you, I don't care about that," Ashli insisted.

"Keep telling me often enough, and perhaps I'll be convinced." He smiled thinly. "What would you like to drink?"

"White wine, please." She watched as Kyle strode over to the bar and placed their order. No matter what the man wore, he always looked terrific, she reflected. Today, it was a simple navy sports shirt and beige slacks. The fine material of the knit shirt accentuated his broad shoulders and hard-muscled chest. Did Mr. Kyle Hamilton ever have a day when he didn't look crisp and neat as an ad in a men's fashion magazine? Didn't his perfectly styled blond hair ever wilt in the summer heat?

Instantly, Ashli felt unattractive in her faded jeans and gray T-shirt. Handsome men like Kyle or beautiful women like Helene would never understand this kind of feeling since they took their exceptional good looks for granted all their lives. In Kyle's case, it had always seemed so effortless for him to maintain the perfection. Right now, she envied the easy conversation he was having with the bartender. Didn't the man ever become nervous and tongue-tied like ordinary mortals?

Kyle returned to the table with a smile. "Your white wine." He placed the glass down in front of her. "Although, I have serious doubts about the vintage."

"I'm sure it will be fine. Thank you, Kyle." She raised the glass to her lips.

"My pleasure," he murmured softly, and immediately took several sips of his Scotch. Right now, Kyle needed that Scotch more than ever. Except for those first couple of years in college, he'd never indulged very much in alcohol, but Ashli's presence was having a dizzying effect on his nerves. "You look very pretty this afternoon," he said, plunging recklessly into conversation. The doubtful expression on her face startled him.

"Why do you say things like that?" she asked, shaking her head in protest.

"Because I mean them."

She shifted uncomfortably in her seat. "Oh, sure."

Kyle was puzzled. His words had been heartfelt and sincere. "Do you think I'm merely being glib?" Impulsively, he reached across the table and grasped her hand. "Haven't enough men told you what an amazingly attractive woman you are?"

Flabbergasted, Ashli gulped her wine. To hear such sweet, warming words from this man brought a flush to her cheeks. Not to mention the effect the delicious touch of his firm hand was having on her. "Not really," she confessed bluntly. "Men haven't exactly been standing in line to compliment me."

"Then all I can say," he responded huskily, "is that all those other men must have needed glasses." It gave Kyle a tantalizing sensation to see Ashli's lower lip quiver.

"I think you're the one who needs a pair of glasses," she remarked nervously.

This wasn't getting him anywhere, Kyle groaned to himself in frustration. And that's when the careless words slipped out of his mouth. "Do you really believe that, Ashli?" he challenged. "Did that egghead professor of yours wear glasses?"

Ashli recoiled as if stung. "Yes," she retorted with a slight tremble in her voice. "Edward wore them."

Kyle immediately regretted his words, but there was no way to take them back now. "Did he ever say nice things to you?"

Her lips thinned. "Certainly. Of course. He often told me how smart I was." She paused. "And how helpful I was in his research. Edward complimented me all the time, I'll have you know."

Kyle downed the rest of his Scotch. "Yes, I'm sure." There was a brief silence. "But did he ever tell you about your eyes?"

"What about my eyes?"

"There are moments when they're not hazel at all—but a deep green."

"Oh" was all Ashli could manage to say. It was so mesmerizing to hear such unexpected words from Kyle.

"Let's have another drink," he muttered hastily, and motioned to the bartender.

"Please, nothing more for me," she protested. It felt strange enough to be sitting in a dimly lit corner listening to Kyle Hamilton talk about the color of her eyes, without confusing her mental circulation any further with a second glass of wine. The first glass was already having a heady effect on her senses.

"When was the last time you had something to eat?" Kyle asked suddenly.

Ashli shrugged. "I don't remember."

"You don't *remember?*"

"Breakfast, I suppose. What does it matter?" In the past few days, she hadn't given much thought to meals. There had been far too many matters of greater importance with which to concern herself.

"It matters," he commented harshly. "Let's get you some dinner."

"That's not necessary."

"Ashli." Kyle reached for her hand again. "I'm supposed to be looking after you."

She was startled. "I beg your pardon?"

He forced a light note into his voice. "What I mean is, your Dad would want me to keep an eye on you."

She tried to ignore the warm tingle from the touch of his hard fingers. "I think you're confusing me with Helene."

A muscle in his jaw tightened. "I could never confuse you with your sister, believe me."

Ashli gave a nervous laugh. "That's not hard to believe. All a person has to do is take one look at my sister and me standing side by side." In Ashli's opinion, it would be like comparing apples with oranges. Helene's icy, blond beauty had always cast a giant shadow over Ashli.

It was almost as if Kyle had read her mind. "Why do you keep comparing yourself to your sister?"

She stared blindly into her wineglass. "Force of habit, I suppose." Kyle Hamilton, of all people, should understand the effect that Helene's golden glow had on others around her. After all, he was one of the golden people himself. "Besides, you should know all about these things," Ashli added dryly. "You and my sister have a lot in common."

There was a pause. "Actually, I was thinking that you and I have a lot more in common, Ashli."

She practically spilled the remainder of her drink. "Are you kidding?"

Abruptly, he released her hand. "Is the idea so unlikely? Can't you imagine that the two of us might have a few common interests?" His eyes narrowed. "Or do you still see me as some superficial dimwit who couldn't possibly stand on equal footing with that professor friend of yours?"

The words were so scathing that Ashli almost reeled in shock. In a stunning reversal of roles, Kyle Hamilton was actually accusing *her* of being a snob. Impulsively, she reached for his hand. "That's not what I meant at all, Kyle!"

He glanced down at her slim fingers where they touched the rough skin of his wrist. "What *do* you mean, then?"

"How can I make you understand?" Ashli questioned him. "It's always been so easy for people like you and Helene. You've always managed to get all the things you've ever wanted."

Kyle looked at her strangely. "Not *all* the things, Ashli."

"I find that hard to believe."

Almost reluctantly, he pulled his hand away, and fumbled in his trouser pocket for his car keys. "Believe whatever you want." He tossed several bills onto the table. "It's painfully obvious that you still don't have the faintest idea about what kind of person I really am."

She stared straight back at him. "If that's true, then perhaps you can enlighten me."

It was Kyle's turn to be startled. "What are you saying, Ashli?"

Maybe it was the wine talking, giving her a rare dose of courage. "I'm saying that I'd like to know you better."

He inhaled sharply. "Exactly *how* much better would you like to know me?"

Chapter Seven

It had seemed such an innocent question, but Ashli suddenly found the blood rushing to her cheeks. How much better would she like to know Kyle? A normal, friendly question between two adults, but Ashli's overactive imagination immediately began conjuring up the most tantalizing images.

There *was* a great deal more she would like to learn about Kyle Hamilton. Such as, what would it feel like to be kissed by that tempting mouth? To have him whisper urgent endearments against her ear? Ashli trembled as she watched the man seated across the table. What would it be like to make love with Kyle Hamilton? She gave an involuntary shiver. In all the years of her infatuation with Edward, she had never felt so physically charged as she felt right now. It was

a completely new sensation, and it was downright unsettling. So unsettling, in fact, that all Ashli wanted to
do at this moment was get as far away as possible from
the Black Swan and her devastatingly attractive companion. She cleared her throat. "I really ought to be
getting home."

He quirked an eyebrow. "It seems to me you're always running away, Ashli."

"No, not at all," she said, attempting a casual tone.
"It's just that it's late."

"We've only been here a short time," he asserted
coolly.

True, Ashli thought with an inward groan, but if she
sat here with Kyle Hamilton much longer, she risked
making a genuine fool of herself. Hastily, she stood
up. "Thanks for the drink, Kyle, but I really have to
go."

He frowned, but didn't offer any further words of
protest. "Fine, I'll walk you to your pickup."

The late-afternoon sun was still hanging brightly in
the August sky as the two of them emerged into the
parking lot. Awkwardly, Ashli thrust open the door of
her yellow pickup truck. "Well, thanks again."

"Anytime." Kyle seemed to hover over her. "In
fact, perhaps next time you won't be in such a hurry."
He raked a hand through his short blond hair. Something seemed to distract him for a moment. "Listen,
Ashli," he said, focussing on her again. "I'd like to be
with you tomorrow when you talk to your father."

Her heart sank. Somehow, during the past half
hour, she had managed to forget the problem of He-

lene. How on earth was she ever going to break the disappointing news to her dad? Ashli gave a resigned sigh. "If you really think your presence will help soften the blow, then I'd appreciate your being there. But the truth is, I don't believe that anything is going to help the situation."

In an unexpectedly gentle gesture, Kyle placed his hands on her shoulders, his warmth burning through the thin material of Ashli's cotton T-shirt. "You're wrong."

"Not about this," she insisted, her system reacting nervously to his touch.

"Why don't you stop worrying?" he queried softly.

"I—I always worry," Ashli stammered. "It's my nature."

"Is that so?" Kyle lowered his mouth to hers in a hard, brief kiss that left her senses spinning.

"Why did you do that?" she breathed in stunned surprise, every inch of her body reeling from the electric contact.

"Perhaps this isn't the best time to answer that question," he replied hoarsely. But his blue eyes betrayed an odd glimmer before he forced himself to turn away hastily and stride across the parking lot to his own car.

Ashli found herself driving past the driveway of the rambling Wilkerson mansion. The last place she wanted to go right now was home. Disbelievingly, she ran a finger across her tender lips. That delicious, tingling sensation brought on by Kyle's unexpected kiss still hadn't faded. She felt shaken and disturbed. At this very moment, Ashli was seized with an urge to visit the one place that had always offered her solace during her teenage days—the place she had always gone when her mind was troubled. Had it really been five years since she had last seen Shadow Lake?

Ashli steered the truck toward the familiar turnoff, and down the curving gravel road. After a few miles, she headed down a narrow dirt track, which was framed with a heavy green canopy of elm trees. About three hundred yards from the water's edge, her eyes were stunned by a newly erected No Trespassing sign.

Ashli shook her head in mild annoyance and decided to ignore the warning. After all, it was late in the afternoon and the area around the lake seemed completely deserted. Except for the rustling of leaves, and a gentle chorus of birds, a sweet and soothing silence encompassed her. Shadow Lake was every bit as clear and tranquil as she had remembered. There was a fresh scent of pine, and a balmy breeze swept across the glittering water.

With a contented half smile, Ashli sat down against a large boulder. It was the same giant rock she had perched upon during her childhood. How reassuring it was that some things never changed. Then, a distressing thought occurred to her. If the Hamiltons had their way, it wouldn't be long before this lovely, unspoiled paradise was defiled in the name of profit and progress. What had Kyle called it? The Shadow Lake Spa and Resort complex. Ashli shuddered at the very idea.

So much had happened in the past week to turn her world topsy-turvy. It wasn't just the shock of her father's sudden illness, or the fact that snooty, fastidious Helene had inexplicably gone off the deep end over an unkempt, struggling artist. Now, hovering in the background of these upsetting developments, was the added problem of Kyle Hamilton.

Kyle. Even now, the realization of what had happened continued to astonish Ashli. After all those years of making fun of the dizzy young females at the country club who had fallen for the charming playboy, she realized she had now joined their ranks. Kyle's kiss had left her a true believer in his charms. How embarrassing to admit that she still felt weak at the knees from the searing imprint of Kyle's mouth. For him, that brief kiss in the parking lot of the Black Swan had probably been a simple, casual gesture; for Ashli, it had changed everything.

During the past five years, the only man who had occupied her thoughts had been Edward. The soft-spoken, gangly, young professor had been a constant presence in her heart and mind. But now, in a matter of an instant, that presence had been permanently eradicated and replaced by something far more intense and powerful. Ashli stared out onto the serene water. Life had become very complicated.

Suddenly, the rustic silence was shattered by the roar of an engine. Ashli turned around apprehensively to see a stocky man on a motorcycle. He wore a red bandana tied around his wide forehead, and a black leather jacket with metal studs. He was staring at her with a cold leer that chilled Ashli right down to the bone.

"Well, now," the motorcyclist said, swinging his legs off the oversize bike, and taking several steps in her direction. "What do we have here?" he inquired with a smirk in his low, gravelly voice.

Instinctively, Ashli stood up and backed away, her heart pounding. Even from this distance, she could sense the danger. Reminding herself to remain calm, Ashli tried to act unperturbed and unafraid. She cleared her throat. "If you don't mind, sir. I came here to be alone."

The man laughed, revealing a gold-capped front tooth. "Well, I guess you ain't alone anymore."

With an increasing surge of panic, Ashli realized she was trapped in a situation that she had so smugly believed she would never find herself in. Alone in a remote location with a stranger whose intentions were now becoming quite horribly clear. "Please, leave me alone," she exclaimed harshly.

He moved closer. "Now, why would I want to do that, honey? I got a better idea—" There was a frightening pause. "You and I are gonna have a party."

Tasting icy fear, Ashli glanced quickly around the narrow strip of beach. There was no place to run and nowhere to escape. Behind her was the water and now the motorcyclist was only inches away. He smelled of sweat and beer. Surely, this had to be some dreadful nightmare! Ashli's tense body seemed paralyzed. She stood there frozen.

"Yeah," he said menacingly, seizing her by the arms roughly. "The two of us are gonna have a *real* good time!"

"Let me go!" She struggled against his barrel chest, but the man was far too strong. His powerful hands were like tight steel bands confining her arms.

"Come on," came the slurred demand, "don't you start playing hard to get!" He brought his ruddy face down to hers.

"No!" Ashli screamed, twisting her head away in revulsion. Suddenly in an instant of brave resolve, she brought her foot down on her assailant's instep.

"Why you—" he howled in pain and anger, raising his fist in the air.

"Don't even think about it!" boomed an ominous voice.

Startled, the motorcyclist's fist froze in midair. "Who the hell are you?" he muttered at the tall, angry figure that had suddenly appeared out of nowhere.

"Let her go—*now!*" the voice commanded harshly.

"Kyle!" Ashli's heart surged with surprise and relief.

Caught off guard, the burly motorcyclist relaxed his grip on her arms and Ashli managed to break free.

"What the—" he began, but before another word could escape his lips, the man was caught in a diving tackle.

Speechless, Ashli stared in astonishment as Kyle and her attacker rolled in the dirt in a vicious tangle. The stocky man outweighed Kyle by at least fifty pounds, but Kyle handled him with a strength and expertise that Ashli had thought he could not possibly possess. Was this the same Kyle Hamilton whose elegant manners and easygoing personality had made him the darling of the country club set? Now, his usually placid features were contorted with rage. His eyes were dark with cold fury. Ashli had never seen Kyle so heroically enraged. Almost like an avenging angel.

"Hey, man," the cyclist pleaded as he gasped for breath, "what are you trying to do, *kill* me?"

"Sounds like a good idea to me," snarled Kyle under his breath, as he delivered another hard left to the man's jaw. "But I'll settle for knocking you out." The man gave a grunt and fell back against the ground, unconscious. Kyle wiped his mouth with satisfaction and slowly rose to his feet.

"Kyle—" Ashli stared at him gratefully.

"Are you all right?" The words seemed torn from his lips.

Ashli nodded mutely. Of course, she was all right. Kyle was here and everything was going to be fine. The fight had left him covered in dust and grime from head to toe. The sleeve of his expensive navy polo shirt was ripped, and his impeccably styled hair was disheveled. In a shattering moment of insight, Ashli realized that no man had ever made her feel so completely safe, so protected.

Kyle reached out angrily and grasped her shoulders. "Do you know what almost happened here? What a narrow escape you just had?" His eyes blazed. "It makes me sick to think what might have happened to you if I hadn't—'' He stopped himself with a shudder.

His hard fingers held her so tightly that Ashli gave an involuntary wince. "It's over. Can't we just forget it?"

"Don't ask me to forget it," Kyle said, his voice actually shaking. "Do you think I can stand the idea of another man touching you?"

She swallowed convulsively. "I didn't think it mattered to you one way or another."

"Oh, it matters," he muttered thickly. "Believe me, it matters." The raw vulnerability in his words was a revelation. "Why the hell didn't you listen when I told you how unsafe this place had become? It's not the same tranquil little spot you remember from your school days, Ashli. And in case you've forgotten how to read, the sign says No Trespassing."

"I know what it says."

A muscle in his jaw tensed. "Ashli, that sign was put up for a reason."

"I'm sure."

Angrily, he drew her against his hard body. "You little fool! Don't you understand that I'm telling you this for your own good?" Kyle almost shook her. "You must never, do you hear me, *never* come here alone again!"

"But I—"

"Never!" he repeated in a harsh whisper.

"You don't understand—" Ashli protested feebly. She gazed up into his glittering blue eyes, and was lost.

"Oh, God!" Kyle groaned before his mouth came down hungrily on hers. It was a kiss that brooked no refusals, as he scorched his brand irrevocably upon her tender lips.

For the first time in her life, Ashli found herself responding eagerly to this devastating assault on her senses.

"Yes, sweetheart," he rasped in amazement, "kiss me back!"

Suddenly torn free of all inhibitions, she sighed against the rough skin of Kyle's cheek and reached up to lock her arms around his neck. It was sheer heaven to be in this man's delicious embrace. Kyle tasted of Scotch and tobacco, his body exuding the distinctly male scent of lime after-shave.

His breath was warm against her mouth. "Kiss me," he whispered again.

With a newfound boldness she had not thought herself capable of, Ashli brushed her lips tentatively against Kyle's own trembling mouth. Trembling, she thought in wonderment. The sophisticated, blasé playboy was actually trembling! Ashli could only marvel as she pressed her soft mouth to his. Kyle's lips suddenly parted, generating an entirely new spectrum of sensation. She pulled back, shaken.

"Don't stop, honey," he pleaded huskily. With a strange new urgency, Kyle brought his hard lips back to hers. Meanwhile, his arms tightened around the small of her back, fitting her slender body even more intimately against his muscular frame.

It was maddening to feel him so close, she thought dizzily. No man had ever held her this way. Even in those five frustrating years of feverish fantasies about Edward, she had never dreamed it was possible to experience such a torrent of exquisite need and desire. It didn't matter where the two of them were, all that mattered was that Kyle go on kissing her.

"Open your mouth for me," he commanded gently. Ashli gave an astonished moan of pleasure as his tongue began to plunder the moist sweetness inside. But in the midst of the delightful sensations that Kyle was coaxing from her eager mouth, a million warning bells were going off in Ashli's mind.

Everything was happening too fast. Just a few days ago, she had been in love with Edward DePaul. Only this afternoon, Kyle Hamilton had been about to marry her own sister. The same man, who now stood clasping her in a passionate embrace, had been willing to walk down the aisle with another woman. Had the world suddenly gone completely crazy? Then, despite all the tender urgings of her traitorous body, Ashli's common sense took over.

"No," she protested faintly, and wrenched herself free.

"What is it?" Kyle asked hoarsely.

"We shouldn't be doing this."

"Yes, we *should.*" His eyes were darkened agates. "We should have done this a long time ago."

"What are you saying?"

He reached back toward her with open arms. "You know what I'm saying, Ashli. The way it's always been between us since that night you came home." Kyle paused thickly. "Come here, honey!"

She swallowed nervously and shook her head. "No, Kyle. This isn't right."

He touched her chin tenderly. "I can't think of anything *more* right." There was a pause. "Tell me you don't feel that way, too."

Ashli averted her eyes. "It doesn't matter what I feel."

Kyle's mouth tightened. "Oh, it matters." He glanced down to where the fallen motorcyclist still lay unconscious in the dirt. "But maybe this isn't the place to talk about it."

Strange, Ashli thought dumbstruck, in the past few moments she'd forgotten all about the biker's presence. Kyle Hamilton had the power to wipe everything else from her mind. And as wonderful as his kiss might feel, the last thing she needed was another man who had such devastating power over her. Especially an experienced lover like Kyle Hamilton who was rumored to have women's hearts for breakfast. "No," she agreed quickly, "this isn't the place."

He traced a tantalizing line across her lower lip with a teasing finger. "Why not come home with me, honey? We can talk there."

Back to the bachelor's lair, Ashli thought dryly. "No, thank you."

He raised an eyebrow. "Running away *again?*"

She shrugged. "Actually, I'm not running. I'm *walking.*"

His hands fell abruptly to his sides. "Fine. Whatever you say." Kyle reached into his trouser pocket for his pack of cigarettes, and flicked his lighter irritably. "It's obvious that you still have a very low opinion of me, Ashli."

"I never had that."

Kyle took a heavy drag of his cigarette. "Oh, you don't have to *say* anything." There was a tense silence. "I know what you think of me."

The nerve of the man, she thought furiously. Acting as though he had personally uncovered her deepest secrets. Of all the conceited, arrogant— Ashli fought for self-control. "You don't know anything about me."

"Sure I do, honey."

"And don't call me *honey!*"

He smiled thinly. "Why not? Is that what your professor called you?"

She bit her lip. "If you must know," she said, her voice tight, "he called me by my name. Ashli."

"Oh, that's right. You prefer men to be inattentive and bloodless," came his acidic retort. "I forgot."

She practically choked. "I don't have to listen to this."

"Fine, run away," Kyle snapped. "That's what you always do, isn't it?"

Ashli could scarcely believe the savagery in his tone. Could this possibly be the same man who had held her so tenderly in his arms just moments before? Could this be the same person who had trembled with each soul-wrenching kiss? "How can you say such a thing to me?" she sputtered in disbelief.

He ripped the cigarette from his mouth and crushed it angrily under his foot. "Do you mean to tell me that it isn't true?"

"I beg your pardon, Mr. Hamilton?" Ashli said, drawing herself up to her full height of five foot six. Never mind that the man still towered over her. "But didn't you just accuse *me* of having a low opinion of *you?* Apparently, it works both ways."

Kyle hesitated, but a black cloud remained across his hard features. "Well, perhaps we both have our blind spots," he conceded glumly.

"Yes," she said, forcing herself to turn away to face her yellow pickup truck. "We do."

"Well, then," he replied caustically. "Better run on home, little girl. You wouldn't want the big bad wolf to get you."

How had everything suddenly changed? Ashli wondered with a pang of regret. She forced herself to sound businesslike. "Thank you for rescuing me from that Neanderthal over there. Goodbye."

Kyle stared past her with unseeing eyes. "Goodbye," he uttered roughly.

For a long while afterward, Kyle continued to stare blindly at the dusty swirl left by the yellow truck after Ashli had sped off into the late afternoon sun.

How could he have been so crazy? Kyle groaned inwardly. It had been going so well, and then he had to act like an utter idiot and blow his top. How could he have been so dense, so stupid to have rushed Ashli that way? And to add to the insanity, what on earth had possibly possessed him to have said all those bitter and nasty things to the one woman he cared so deeply about? He had to be off his rocker, Kyle chided himself harshly. Kissing her had been the closest thing to heaven, but his petty jealousy over her relationship with Edward DePaul had ruined everything.

Damn, Kyle cursed himself. There was absolutely no way Ashli would want him now. And soon she would be gone. Unless he thought of something drastic to stop her from going. Something to buy him the time in which to win Ashli's heart before she disappeared from his life.

Chapter Eight

All the way home, Ashli shivered as over and over again she relived the disturbing encounter with Kyle Hamilton. She had limited experience with the opposite sex. It didn't take much experience, however, to realize that the chemistry between her and Kyle was undeniable. In truth, she had run away from him because their burgeoning intimacy astonished and frightened her. It would have been so easy to submit to the clamoring need she felt at his touch. He was so sure of himself, so confident—Ashli knew a man like him could hurt her more deeply than Edward DePaul ever had.

The shattering vulnerability awakened by Kyle's persuasive kisses had driven that point home sharply this afternoon at Shadow Lake. The vicious motor-

cyclist had left her shaken and terrified, but Kyle had
not only rescued her from a terrible fate—he had irrevocably placed his stamp of ownership on her. She
had become angry and defensive because Kyle had
unwittingly guessed the truth. She *was* running away.
Running away from something more dangerous than
she had ever known. Something so potentially explo-
sive Ashli dared not name it. But why not face facts?
The handsome playboy was a part of her now, despite
how she might try to deny it. Her heart had a will of
its own, and she knew she was coming perilously close
to falling in love with Kyle Hamilton.

Greatly upset by this realization, Ashli skidded
recklessly to a stop in the center of the huge, circular
driveway in front of her father's house. To her surprise, Charles was standing at the bottom step, his
crisp white jacket wilted and a bewildered expression
on his usually imperturbable face.

"Miss Ashli!" he exclaimed with considerable chagrin.

Hastily, she hopped out of the truck. "What's
wrong, Charles?"

With a wiry arm, he held out a neatly folded piece
of paper. "Miss Helene told me to give this to you."
He paused significantly. "She's gone! She left the
house several hours ago. And she took only *one* suit-
case!"

Silently, Ashli took the note. So her sister had really gone ahead and done it. She unfolded the square
of paper.

Dear Ash,

I've gone with Simon to Vermont. Wish me luck and tell Father not to be mad.

Love, Helene

Strange, now that it had actually happened, Ashli found it hard to believe that her older sister had found the courage.

"She told me of her plans," Charles murmured. "And quite frankly, I'm astonished."

"I can see that," Ashli commented dryly.

"This type of irresponsible behavior is so *unlike* Miss Helene!" the butler insisted. "How in the world are we ever going to explain this to your father?" Charles seemed truly distressed. Andrew Wilkerson's unexpected illness had hit him especially hard. The middle-aged man had served the wealthy businessman devotedly for thirty years.

"We'll just have to break it to him gently," she said in a soft voice.

Charles remained apprehensive. "Miss Ashli, your father is not a well man."

"If it makes any difference, Kyle has asked to be here when we tell him."

Charles gave her a penetrating look. "Has he?"

"Why are you looking at me like that?"

"Like *what*, Miss Ashli?" Charles asked innocently.

The expression on his face was cryptic, but Ashli had long since given up trying to read his mind.

"Oh, forget it!" she said, sighing in exasperation. Still, something infinitely wise in the depths of Charles's gray eyes continued to puzzle her. It was not until much later that Ashli would discover the answer: When it came to matters involving Kyle Hamilton, Charles possessed an extraordinary sixth sense.

They brought her father home from the hospital the next morning, and from the moment he was back in his huge master bedroom overlooking the garden, Andrew seemed to be his old self again, grumbling and barking out orders.

"Where are all my cigars?" he complained gruffly to Charles.

"I've discarded them all in the trash, sir," the butler answered coolly.

"Why, you blazing, incompetent—"

"Daddy," Ashli said, giving her father a stern look, "Charles is only following your doctor's orders."

"All doctors are fools!" the older man muttered irritably. "You didn't *really* throw my wonderful, hand-rolled panatelas in the garbage, did you, Charles?"

"No, sir. I have them in my room, and you're quite right. They're excellent cigars."

"I'm surrounded by scoundrels!" Andrew groaned to his daughter, but Ashli knew it was little more than an act. Her father had the greatest respect for Charles Wingate.

"Remember, you're not supposed to get excited," she urged, touching his shoulder affectionately.

"Hmmph! How can a man get along without his cigars?"

"I suggest you consider lollipops, sir," the butler offered.

This little argument went on for about ten minutes, and Ashli was grateful that the temporary distraction drew her father's attention away from the fact that Helene was nowhere in sight. Ashli dreaded the moment she would have to reveal the truth.

"I rang the bell, but nobody answered," Kyle said, suddenly towering in the doorway of Andrew's bedroom.

Ashli's heart gave an involuntary lurch, while her father beamed delightedly from his enormous oak bed. "Well, if it isn't my son-in-law-to-be!"

Oh, Lord, she thought warily as her eyes locked with Kyle's. Now was the moment they would have to tell him. Kyle seemed unusually tense, too. She cleared her throat nervously. "It's good to see you, Kyle."

He arched an eyebrow. "Is it?" With words unspoken, Kyle seemed to be asking her a question. And yet, he also seemed to be apologizing for something. Was it Ashli's imagination, or was there a regretful look in those bright blue eyes?

Once again, Charles glanced at Ashli, then at Kyle, and then back at Ashli again. "If you will excuse me, I'll attend to lunch."

"None of that damn broth, do you hear me?" grumbled Andrew. "Give me a steak, medium rare."

"You'll have a chicken sandwich and consommé," came the bland retort as Charles exited the room.

"I should have fired you years ago!" her father roared after him. He looked at Kyle beseechingly. "Couldn't you rustle me up a few cheeseburgers from the Black Swan?"

Kyle laughed lightly. "Maybe later. Right now, I was wondering if we could have a little chat." He hesitated and glanced at Ashli. "I'd like to speak with Andrew alone."

"Alone?" she said in surprise. What was Kyle up to, anyway? Hadn't they agreed to tell her father the bad news about the broken engagement together?

Kyle tore his eyes reluctantly from Ashli. She looked so beautiful this morning in that simple yellow T-shirt and those snug jeans, it made him feel downright self-conscious. He'd stayed awake all night building up the resolve to say what he was about to say to Andrew Wilkerson. He knew he was taking a terrible risk. Ashli might very well despise him for it, but he knew that was the chance he had to take. Kyle forced himself to ignore Ashli's puzzled hazel eyes and to look only at Andrew. "Yes, there's a matter I'd like to discuss with you in private."

"You heard the young man, dear," her father said impatiently. "This is a private discussion."

"Very well," she said, nodding uneasily. She paused to glance at Kyle, but he made a strict point of averting his eyes, unwilling to meet her curious gaze. Ashli sighed, walking from the bedroom with a rueful expression on her face, and shut the door behind her.

Five minutes went by, then ten minutes, and then another ten minutes. All in all, nearly half an hour elapsed before Kyle opened the bedroom door and strode quietly down the carpeted hallway to where Ashli sat waiting in the gabled window seat overlooking the driveway.

"Did you tell him?"

There was an odd light in Kyle's eyes. "Yes, I told him."

"Well?"

"Well, what?"

She stood up impatiently. "How did he take it?"

"Actually, your father took it quite well," he replied tautly.

Relief flooded Ashli. "Thank goodness! That's wonderful!"

"I wouldn't jump to any conclusions, yet. After all, you don't know exactly what I told your father."

"Well, whatever you said, it must have worked like a charm. I believe I can actually hear Dad chuckling all the way down the corridor." Despite the fact that the man still made her feel a bit shy and nervous, Ashli gave Kyle a dazzling smile.

It was the kind of smile that he had always dreamed of receiving. It was the kind of smile that sent sweet shivers down his spine. At any other time, Kyle would have been overwhelmed with delight, but at this moment, when he revealed the truth of his actions to Ashli, the bright warmth in her eyes would turn to cold shock and outrage. Oh, yes, Kyle thought guiltily, there was a good reason why Andrew Wilkerson now sat bewildered but blissfully content in his sickbed. And that reason certainly had nothing at all to do with

Helene's having run away with a penniless sculptor to the wilds of Vermont.

He cleared his throat. "Listen, Ashli," he began awkwardly, "about what I said to your father..."

"Hmm?"

"You see, he was pretty upset when he learned that your sister had suddenly broken our engagement—" Kyle stopped. *Now* he would see Ashli's sweet smile turn to ice.

Confused, Ashli asked, "Then, why is he laughing?"

Kyle drew a deep breath. "Andrew looked so crushed and shattered after I broke the news about Helene, I was convinced he was about to have a relapse. *That's* when I told him..." there was just the briefest instant of hesitation "...that you and I had decided to get married instead."

There was a stunned silence. "You told him *what?*"

"I told him the two of us were getting married," Kyle repeated solemnly.

"Is this some kind of a joke?" The words almost caught in her throat.

Kyle stood stiffly, preparing himself for the worst possible reaction. He shook his head. "It's no joke, Ashli."

"Do you mean to tell me," she asked, her voice barely audible, "you care so much about my father that you would actually be willing to marry *me* to make *him* happy?"

He forced a casual shrug. "It's not such a bad idea, is it? I mean, the two of us seem rather compatible, and it would keep things in the family, after all."

The brief moment of hope washed away. "Oh," Ashli said, lowering her eyes. "I see. In other words, one sister is pretty much the same as the other."

The bitterness in her words astonished Kyle. "Believe me, that's not it at all."

"Then what is it, exactly?" The blood was racing to Ashli's head.

He folded his arms confidently. "You needn't sound so annoyed, Ashli. In most circles, I happen to be considered quite a catch."

She twisted her lips. "So I've heard."

"Frankly, you could do a lot worse than marry me, you know."

Of all the nerve, Ashli fumed indignantly. "Why you pompous, stuck-up jerk! You make it sound as though you're doing me some kind of enormous favor!"

Kyle's expression was bland. "I'm not doing you a favor, Ashli. I'm simply stating a fact. All things considered, you're not likely to get a better offer than me."

"Thank you so very much," came her icy retort.

He flinched. What on earth had he expected Ashli's reaction to be, anyhow? Had he seriously overrated his charms where this lovely young creature was concerned? It wasn't conceit, it was a simple fact that women had always found him irresistible before. But now that he'd finally found the one he desperately

wanted to share his life with, Kyle had ended up bun-
gling his proposal completely. Oh, he had expected
Ashli to be angry and shocked, but the one thing he
hadn't expected was that she'd be downright insulted.
"It's not what you think, at all," Kyle explained
lamely as a muscle in his jaw tensed.

Two bright spots of outrage bloomed on her cheeks.
"Oh, I think it's *exactly* the way you meant it." She
paused to stare at him coldly. "People like yourself,
Jonas, and my own father view marriage as just another business deal. As far as you're concerned, the
deal should go through, whether it's one Wilkerson
sister or another."

"I never said that."

"But you meant it, so what's the difference?" Ashli
had never been so angry. She took a step toward this
new nemesis and placed her hands on her hips defiantly. "It was a real dirty trick, Mr. Kyle Hamilton—
making sure I was out of the room when you 'broke
the news' to my father. You've put me into a terrible
position."

He arched an eyebrow. "I wouldn't call it *terrible*,
Ashli. Who knows?" he observed, smiling thinly.
"You might even enjoy being married to me."

For just a moment, Ashli felt a traitorous tingle
shoot through her knees at the thought of being married to Kyle. At the thought of Kyle's sure hands
touching her body— *No*. She stopped the stirrings
which had almost betrayed her secret heart. Kyle had
put forth a cold business proposition, pure and simple. Love, or even passion, did not enter into the

equation as far as he was concerned. Irritably, Ashli
tossed back her mane of glossy, brown hair. "I very
much doubt that being married to you would be particularly enjoyable, Mr. Hamilton," she lied.

"How do you know unless you give it half a
chance?" he taunted her.

"Spare me."

"I suppose you realize how terribly disappointed
your father is going to be now. And what a shame,
too," Kyle said, trying to sound ruthless, "after I'd
gone to all that trouble to finally convince him that
Helene had found true love, and that you and I had
decided we were far more compatible, anyway." He
twisted his lips. "But go right ahead, Ashli. You go in
and tell your father that it was all a mistake and the
wedding is off."

"Of all the rotten, conniving—"

"Temper, temper," Kyle teased, and reached into
his pocket for a pack of cigarettes. "Honestly, Ashli.
I think you're taking this entire marriage thing far too
seriously." Oh, Lord, Kyle was thinking in a near
panic, how much longer could he maintain this cool
facade? With dazzling incompetence, he'd completely botched everything. Why couldn't he have just
come out and told Ashli the true depth of his feelings
for her? Why was he so damned afraid of making a
fool of himself? By not telling her how he felt about
her, he'd succeeded in making Ashli despise him, Kyle
groaned inwardly. How had he ever managed to have
dug himself such a great big hole?

"How could you have done something so despicable to me, Kyle?" Ashli tried to fight the frustration and tears that were starting to well in her hazel eyes. "I thought we were friends. I thought...you liked me."

"Of course, I like you," Kyle muttered heavily, the poignancy in Ashli's words ripping straight through his own heart. And then he saw the tears. "Lord, don't cry, honey!" With a muffled oath, he pulled her roughly into his arms. "Please don't cry," Kyle repeated against the flushed skin of her forehead.

"I'm not crying!" She tried to struggle out of his tight grasp, but Kyle refused to let her budge.

"Listen to me, Ashli—"

"I don't want to listen to you."

Gently, he cupped her chin. "You're going to listen anyway. I've made a mess of things, but maybe it's not too late to clear things up."

"Clear what things up?" She attempted to avert his intense gaze.

"Do you honestly believe that I'd only marry you because of business?"

"Absolutely. Wasn't that why you were so eager to marry Helene?"

He drew a breath. "*That* was different."

"Why?"

"Why?" Kyle felt the lightness rushing through his heart. *Because I love you,* he wanted to shout aloud. But he stifled the words before they could betray his emotions. He wasn't ready to go that far, to tell Ashli how he truly felt. He had never in his life told a woman that he loved her. He couldn't risk the chance of Ashli leaving Elm Grove and walking out of his life, forever.

There had been no time to woo her in the traditional way—slowly, gently, before she was even aware of what was happening. Flowers, moonlit dinners, and walks by the lake. There was no time for any of that, and he had panicked.

It wasn't just Ashli's adorable body that obsessed him, but her heart and mind, as well. So this was what it felt like to love someone, to experience such a hunger for total possession. But Kyle had waited thirty-five years and now his usually confident demeanor deserted him. Trying to ignore the feel of her soft, slender body in his arms, Kyle struggled for the right words that would answer Ashli's bewildered stare. "There's a twelve-year age difference between us," he said, his voice suddenly raw and vulnerable. "Is thirty-five too old for you?"

"No," she replied, glancing at him in surprise. "Your age never entered my mind."

"Are you sure?"

"Quite sure." Ashli still couldn't believe this was happening.

"I'm glad. Let me make this quite plain, Ashli. I *want* to marry you. And business has absolutely nothing to do with it."

Ashli trembled involuntarily. "What are you saying to me?"

"This." His arms traveled further around Ashli's waist, drawing her up even more tightly to his hard, athletic frame. "This is the difference. *This* is why we belong together, sweetheart."

The gentle endearment clutched at her stomach. "But Kyle," she said, trying to sound calm and unperturbed, "I don't think—"

"Stop thinking, Ashli." His breath fanned her hot cheek. "Stop being sensible, logical, and scientific and just let me touch you!"

It was difficult to think straight when he was holding her so close. His warmth, his strength, and the heady masculine scent of him made Ashli tremble straight down to the marrow. And the look in Kyle's eyes was almost enough to stop a woman's heart.

"Don't you understand?" he rasped against the tender flesh of her earlobe. "Can't you feel how it is between us, little one? The way it's been since that first moment on the staircase?"

"But you were going to marry Helene!" Ashli tried to resist the exotic languor that had slowly invaded her limbs and was threatening to engulf her senses.

"Oh, baby, forget Helene!" Kyle growled before his hungry mouth claimed hers in a shattering kiss. Firm hands molded Ashli's hips to his in a shockingly intimate embrace. "Just feel what you do to me!" he groaned.

So this was what it was like to be wanted by a man. Wanted so badly that someone as strong as Kyle could actually shiver in her arms. Locked in the burning heat of electric contact, Ashli felt a thrill of excitement. It was an overpowering sensation that reduced the memory of her feelings for Edward DePaul to a mere schoolgirl crush. Just a frail, wispy shadow of what she felt for Kyle. This was how love truly felt.

Love, the realization washed over her with astonished relief. Why had she fought against it so tenaciously? Ashli loved this man with her entire heart and soul. She loved Kyle Hamilton, and despite the tarnished circumstances, every nerve in her body silently screamed, "Yes, I want to marry you!" More than anything else in the world, she ached to accept Kyle's proposal. To do all the things that a husband and wife did together. Not just the undeniably delightful prospect of making love, but also the simple, everyday little things that married couples did. Sharing confidences with each other, having morning coffee at the table, and all the Christmas Eves and Thanksgivings that would have an even greater meaning because they would be a family. *A family.* Ashli's spirits soared crazily. Oh, yes, she wanted more than anything to have this man's children. Kyle would be a marvelous father.

"Say something. Anything!" he pleaded, an odd tension in his eyes.

Ashli swallowed convulsively and buried her face in his shoulder. "What do you want me to say?" came her barely audible reply.

"Just say 'yes,' Ashli," he returned in a strained whisper. "Just agree to go through with this wedding."

This was crazy. This was totally insane. Absolute insanity, Ashli chastised her fluttering heart. A man she hardly knew had asked her to marry him less than a day after his engagement to her own sister had been broken. Yet, as a million warning bells went off in her head, the traitorous response was already passing through Ashli's lips. "Yes." She raised her head and pierced Kyle's troubled blue gaze with a tremulous smile. "I'll marry you." *Madness!*

Relief flooded his hard face. "You won't regret this, I promise." In one swift motion, Kyle picked Ashli up in his arms and carried her back to the window seat, settling her across his knees against the soft, paisley cushions. "You'll never be sorry," he murmured, as he ran a deliberate, tantalizing finger across the scoop neckline of her thin, cotton T-shirt.

Ashli quivered in surprise as Kyle's hand brushed for an exquisite instant along the exposed hollow between her breasts. "Are you sure you really want to go through with this?" she managed to finally say.

"I've always been sure." He pressed his lips possessively to the base of her throat. It excited him to feel the heightened flutter of her pulse. "You're going to belong to me," Kyle breathed.

I've always belonged to you, she cried out silently. Ashli knew with bittersweet irony that the feelings she had for this man were stronger than those he had for her, but somehow, at the moment, that didn't seem to matter. At least Kyle wanted her, desired her with an urgency that could not be denied. He had not mentioned love once. Perhaps, that would come in time. Meanwhile, Ashli tried to block out the faint ache in her disappointed heart. Her love would just have to be strong enough for both of them. "Just touch me, Kyle," she blurted out breathlessly.

His entire body shuddered in amazement. "I'll touch you everywhere, darling," he agreed thickly, and pushed her backward against the cushions. "Everywhere!" The words were buried in a trail of liquid fire over her eyelids, cheeks, and mouth, his lips plucking the sweetness from within the tender moistness. Kyle's tongue taunted and teased her with experienced mastery. He was teaching her a new and urgent response with every maddening caress.

Ashli reached up and wound her arms eagerly around Kyle's neck, straining to get closer, much closer than they were now. She quivered again, knowing that it was heaven enough to be touched with such exquisite possession. After so many years of waiting. A lifetime. Despite her lamentably limited experience with the opposite sex, Ashli was flooded with the delicious knowledge that when the time came this man would guide her confidently down the path of total physical fulfillment.

Kyle lifted up the silky curtain of hair that tumbled around her shoulders, and pressed his heated mouth against the sensitive skin at the nape of her neck. "Like velvet," he murmured huskily. "Sweet velvet, honey!" Boldly, his hand moved up over Ashli's rib cage and then higher, cupping one rounded breast.

"Kyle!" Her eyes widened in shocked pleasure.

A muscle in his jaw tensed. "We'd better have the wedding damn soon, I'd say." With a muffled oath, he pulled his hand away reluctantly and forced himself to slide out from underneath her and stand up. But he could not conceal the raw hunger in his glittering eyes as he stared down at Ashli. She half lay, half sat upon the window seat, her mouth still moist and open from Kyle's kisses, and her hair in shiny, alluring disarray. "Somehow," he breathed heavily, "I know just what you'll look like when we finally make love."

"Don't talk like that." She blushed bright crimson, lowering her eyes in embarrassment.

"Ashli," he said, pulling her up gently into his strong arms. "Don't ever be shy with me." Kyle brushed a stray wisp of hair from her cheek. "There's nothing to be embarrassed about."

Hastily, she averted her eyes. There was no way Kyle could understand that her awkwardness was completely justified. Even now, while his touch excited her, she felt secretly mortified about her own inexperience. A man like Kyle must have made love to dozens of women—so how could Ashli ever explain to him that even after twenty-three years, she had never known intimacy with any man? "I'm not embarrassed," she lied. He mustn't know. She couldn't bear the humiliation of revealing to Kyle her total lack of experience. It was far too deep, far too personal.

"I hope not," he replied firmly. Kyle caught her mouth in a hard, brief kiss. "You're really something, do you know that?" Wrenching himself away with a groan, he ran an unsteady hand through his disheveled blond hair. "I suppose we'd both better go and talk to Andrew now." He hesitated. "You aren't going to change your mind, are you?"

"No." Ashli shook her head numbly. Events seemed completely beyond her control. What on earth had happened to her logical, scientific brain during the past few weeks? And now, she had actually agreed to marry a man who didn't even love her. A million alarm bells should be going off in Ashli's head right at this moment, but instead, she was thinking how sensible this decision truly was. Historically, arranged marriages were always the most successful. One sister taking another's place at the altar was nothing unusual.

There was an eerie, dreamlike quality to everything that happened between herself and Kyle. Meanwhile, this wedding would please her father greatly. After all these years of being an absent daughter, Ashli at least owed him that much. And as far as Kyle not being in love with her—well, Ashli gave a pained sigh. If she waited for a man to fall in love with her, she might wait forever. Why let herself rot on the vine? came the bitter realization. No man had ever told Ashli he loved her, and perhaps no man ever would. It was probably time she accepted this fact, and settled for the one-sided love she felt for Kyle. At least, he desired her. Maybe life wasn't supposed to be perfect.

Chapter Nine

An almost bizarre air of unreality hung over the whole day. First there was the stunned reaction of Andrew Wilkerson to the incredible change of events.

"I don't know what to say, dear," he had said, gazing at Ashli quietly from his bed. "I had no idea that Helene was so unhappy. I wasn't trying to force your sister into anything she didn't want."

"Never mind, Dad," Ashli said gently. "I'm sure she's ecstatically happy now."

A slow smile spread across her father's face. "I've been a blind fool in many ways. I never realized that while Jonas and I were busy plotting the wedding of the century, you and Kyle had fallen in love."

"What?" Ashli's voice caught in her throat.

"Oh, now don't blush so, dear. I admit I was a little surprised myself, but when I gave it more thought, everything made perfect sense. Opposites attract. It's actually quite logical that the two of you are in love."

Hope flared in her heart. "Did Kyle tell you that?"

Andrew shrugged. "Nobody has to tell me anything. I just *know*."

The flicker of hope evaporated instantly. "Well, in any event," Ashli said, concealing her bitter disappointment with a bright smile, "the important thing is that you're getting better every day. Dr. Montrose says he's simply amazed."

"There's nothing amazing about it at all, child," her father said, placing a hand over hers. "Your marrying Kyle has made all the difference in the world to me. Lord help me for playing favorites with my daughters, but it's what I've secretly prayed for all along. I never dreamed that you would agree to settle down in Elm Grove."

Yes, Ashli thought, perhaps it was all worth it, just to see the bloom of complete happiness on her father's face. Even if it meant she would be letting herself in for inevitable pain and frustration being married to a wonderful man who had, nonetheless, never mentioned the word *love*.

For an instant, Andrew seemed alarmed. "Well, say something. You've become terribly quiet all of a sudden."

"Have I?"

"You haven't changed your mind, Ashli?"

Hastily, she gave a contrived laugh. "No, of course not, Dad!"

"Then why the strange expression on your face?"

"No, not at all!" There was a pause. "I was just thinking that with Helene not marrying Kyle, you aren't going to have such gorgeous grandchildren, after all."

He grinned. "Who can tell, Ashli? With a combination like you and Kyle, you'll probably have the feistiest, most irritatingly independent babies in the world. Just like their grandpa."

"Oh." Just the thought of having a baby with Kyle sent a tingle along Ashli's spine, in spite of all her other misgivings.

Andrew positively glowed. He bore no resemblance to the stricken old man who had lain with tubes and monitors surrounding him in the hospital bed just a week before. He actually appeared twenty years younger. "Don't put off having children, like so many young couples of your generation, dear. I can't wait to be a grandfather, and Jonas intends to spoil those babies rotten!"

Leaving her father looking absolutely blissful, Ashli went back downstairs, her mind troubled by a thousand disturbing thoughts.

That afternoon, Kyle and Jonas Hamilton came over to the house. Andrew, his health vastly improved, spent several hours in his burnished leather lounge chair, chattering away with his boyhood chum. Both older men were excitedly occupied with plans for the wedding and the future of their children. Kyle just sat quietly next to Ashli on the small sofa on the other side of Andrew's spacious bedroom. He held her hand in a reassuring gentle grip.

"Don't pay any attention to them," he remarked softly. "As far as I'm concerned, we're going to elope."

Ashli nodded. "That's fine with me."

"Elope? Never!" boomed both fathers in outrage.

"What do you think?" Kyle's penetrating blue eyes searched Ashli's guarded face.

"I don't want a big wedding."

"I agree. And the truth is," Kyle said, turning matter-of-factly toward the two other men, "considering the circumstances, a simple private ceremony is the sensible thing to have."

There was an awkward silence, and then, Jonas nodded. "The boy is quite right, I suppose. It seems like just the other day that the entire town was here to celebrate Kyle and Helene's engagement. I agree that a lavish wedding might not be in the . . . best of taste."

A brief expression of pain flickered across Andrew's ruddy features. "Maybe not," he finally conceded.

Kyle cleared his throat, and stood up abruptly. "If you'll excuse us, I'd like to discuss a few things with my fiancée."

Just hearing that word made Ashli give an involuntary start. For a moment, she actually wondered whom Kyle was talking about. That's me, she thought with odd wonderment. I'm Kyle Hamilton's fiancée.

In a daze, she slowly stood up, nodded to her father and Jonas, then allowed Kyle to lead her from the room.

In the hallway, he towered over Ashli, a tense look on his rugged face. "Say something."

"About what?"

"Anything."

She stared up at him in puzzlement. "I don't understand—"

Kyle folded his arms. "All right, I confess I've pushed you into this engagement," he stated quietly. "Are you as indifferent to me as you seemed tonight?"

"I'm not indifferent to you, Kyle."

"Then show me how you really feel." His hands came down firmly on the soft, white sweater material covering her shoulders. "You haven't kissed me in hours. Not since I asked you to marry me, Ashli."

She bit her lip. "I believe you *told* me I was going to marry you."

"Whatever," Kyle uttered roughly, and lowered his mouth to hers.

He tasted of tobacco and after-dinner brandy. Ashli instinctively yielded her body to his, and opened her mouth to the hungry, urgent probings of Kyle's tongue.

"Yes," he breathed harshly against her parted mouth. "Like that!" Kyle lowered his hands possessively to her hips and pulled Ashli closer to his own hard, muscled strength.

She felt breathless and wanton, her unpracticed body craving more than the limited confines of his teasing embrace. Boldly, Ashli planted whisper-soft kisses along the tense line of Kyle's jaw, down to where a tiny vein throbbed in his neck. "Like that?" she inquired silkily.

"Are you trying to torture me?" He gave a half groan, half laugh.

"I didn't start this!"

"No, I suppose not." Kyle's tanned face seemed so animated and boyish. "It's my own fault for wanting to get you alone like this. Can I help it if you look so damn adorable tonight?" A proprietary finger ran lightly across Ashli's scoop neckline. "Hmm, what is this material, anyway?"

The brush of his fingertip along the hollow between her breasts gave Ashli tiny goosebumps. "Angora," she whispered shakily against the open collar of his cotton polo shirt.

"Angora?" he murmured thickly. "It's so soft and sweet, just like you, honey. When we're married, remind me to buy you a boxload of angora sweaters."

"You don't have to buy me anything."

Kyle lightly pressed his thumb to her lips and turned Ashli's face up toward his own. "I *want* to buy you everything," he said huskily, an odd catch in the back of his throat. "That's a husband's prerogative, might I remind you, Ashli. A man enjoys giving his wife all kinds of frivolous, silky things." Kyle paused. "But you'll find that out on our honeymoon."

She tried unsuccessfully to stifle a quiver. "Don't waste your time," she retorted casually. "I'm strictly a flannel pajamas kind of girl."

"We'll soon see about that," he growled into her ear. "We'll soon see!" With an amused smile, Kyle brushed a shiny brown strand of hair away from her cheek and gently bit her earlobe.

"Kyle!"

"Don't you like it when I touch you there, honey?"

"It makes me feel out of control," Ashli confessed with a red flush coloring her cheeks.

His eyes glimmered bright blue. "Oh, baby, that's just what I wanted to hear." Wickedly, Kyle's hand slipped beneath the fluffy, knit material and touched the bare skin of her midriff. "When it happens between us at last, it's going to be so perfect, Ashli." All at once, the laughter left his voice, and he stared at her in dead earnestness. "I'll make it so perfect, you'll forget every other man."

Was it her imagination, or was there actually a tinge of desperation in Kyle's tone? Ashli stared back at him in momentary disbelief. *Now* was the time to tell him, she thought. Now was the moment to confess that there had never been any lovers before in her life, and that when she and Kyle at last made love on their wedding night, it would be her first time with any man. "Kyle," she began tentatively. It was both frightening and embarrassing to have to make such a confession.

"What is it?" He was suddenly alert.

"I have something to tell...I mean, *explain* to you."
Lord, this was difficult, Ashli groaned inwardly.

"What is it?" Kyle repeated, the lines of tension
reappearing on his face. He was suddenly afraid. The
look on Ashli's face was so solemn, so serious. Was
she going to confess that she was still deeply in love
with that brilliant professor of hers? A sharp pain
stabbed through Kyle's heart. Anything but that, he
thought in a blind, white-hot panic. *Please don't let it
be that.* "What do you want to tell me?" he asked,
grinding out the words with harsh reluctance.

Ashli stared past him, at the patterned wallpaper. At
the antique silver sconce her father had brought home
from Paris years before. Anything to distract herself
from the excruciating awkwardness of this moment
with Kyle. In a short space of days, the man had
stripped bare so many layers of her heart and soul—
still, in many ways they were virtually strangers. To
even discuss her sexual experience was embarrassing,
perhaps even humiliating, as well. Uncomfortably, she
looked back into Kyle's narrowed eyes. "It's just...it's
just that I'm not—"

"You're not what?" The words dragged out of his
mouth.

I'm not the experienced woman you think I am!
Ashli wanted to cry out, but at that moment, all her
courage evaporated. She cleared her throat. "I'm not
going to give up my studies just because we're getting
married."

"That's fine." Kyle actually seemed relieved. "I'd never ask you to give up your career, Ashli. No man has the right to ask that of any woman."

Actually, the pursuit of her doctorate degree was the furthest thing from Ashli's mind at the moment. The disillusionment over Edward, her father's sudden illness, and the devastating force of her newfound love for Kyle Hamilton had washed over Ashli like a tidal wave. It had swept away all her common sense. True, the fall semester was gone, and working toward a doctorate entailed a great deal of time and commitment. But that was all still her own decision to make. A decision that suddenly did not seem all that urgent. After five years of burying her face in books, maps, and diagrams, Ashli decided that it was time to stop and smell the roses, as the old expression went.

"In fact," Kyle continued now, "I have a proposition I'd like to make to you."

She arched an eyebrow. "A proposition?"

He gave a faint smile. "It's not what you think. Although—" Kyle's hand reached out and traced a delicate line along her lower lip "—right now, that seems like an excellent idea, too." He felt Ashli tremble beneath the light touch of his fingertip, and gave a groan. "You're doing it again, Ashli!"

"Doing what?"

"You know very well *what!*" His voice thickened. "You're distracting me, honey." With obvious effort, Kyle reluctantly drew back his hand. "You're always a distraction. That's the effect you seem to have on me."

A shiver of delicious wonderment washed over her. "Do I?" Ashli still couldn't believe she could have that kind of power over a man, any man. Especially someone as confident and in control as Kyle Hamilton. "Are you teasing me?"

"Teasing, *hell!*" He raked a hand through his hair. "Later on, I'll show you just how much I'm teasing you, Miss Ashli Wilkerson." There was a brief pause. "But right at the moment, I'd better tell you about my business proposition before you drive all the practical, mundane thoughts out of my mind."

"What kind of business are you talking about, Kyle?"

"Well, it's about the Shadow Lake Project." He hesitated again. "After our little *discussion* at dinner last week, I started to do a great deal of thinking about the possible historical significance of the area around the lake. Once the earth-moving equipment starts excavating the site, who knows what artifacts the workers might uncover?"

"I could have told you that," she retorted dryly.

"Well, that's where *you* come in, honey."

"Me?"

"I realize you don't approve of the development—"

Ashli shrugged. "Let's just say I'm not sure exactly how I feel." In truth, after the frightening incident with the vicious biker at the lake, Ashli had begun to see Kyle's point of view. As enchanted and wonderful as Shadow Lake had been during her childhood, it had become apparent that things had certainly deteriorated over the years.

"Well," he went on complacently, "then perhaps my idea will meet with your approval. I'd like you to consider spending whatever available time you can spare to be a consultant after the ground-breaking starts."

"Are you serious?" Ashli asked incredulously.

"Very serious." Kyle sighed. "As I've already said, you have quite an effect on me. Perhaps, there might be some value in keeping a link with Elm Grove's Indian heritage. Considering your longtime interest in the area, along with your academic background, you'd be exactly the right person for the job."

"I don't know what to say." Ashli was frankly mystified.

"Just say 'yes.'"

"Of course, I'll say 'yes,' Kyle," she answered quickly. "It's just that I never thought you were particularly interested in preserving any aspect of Elm Grove's history."

"There's a lot about me that you don't know," he replied in a deliberately bland tone.

"Is that so?" she challenged softly. "Such as?"

Kyle's gaze was cool blue. "Why don't we continue this discussion at dinner?"

"Dinner?"

He shook his head in mild amusement. "*Dinner,* Ashli. That's the meal people eat after lunch and before breakfast."

"I know what it is."

Kyle inclined his head. "I thought we'd go to the club." A silence ensued. "We're engaged, Ashli, and we still haven't had a real date yet."

"Oh." What else could she say?

Kyle noted Ashli's luminous hazel eyes. "A *real* date—" he said meaningfully, "dinner, dancing, champagne... the whole nine yards."

The thought of a slow dance in the arms of Kyle filled her with delectable anticipation, but it also made Ashli distinctly uncomfortable. "I don't think it would be a very good idea."

"Why not?"

"Well, because Daddy just came home today, and I have no intention of leaving him alone."

"He wouldn't be alone," Kyle asserted. "My father and Charles will both be here, and in the unlikely event that something should come up, they can reach us at the country club." He paused for a moment. "Besides," he added silkily, "Andrew would really like to see the two of us all dressed up and out on the town. He's mentioned it several times already."

She was surprised. "He has?"

"Sure," he countered suavely. "He told me just this afternoon that it's been over five years since he's seen you in an evening dress. I honestly believe it would mean quite a lot to him."

Ashli remained silent for a long moment. "Do you really think it's a good idea to be seen in public together so soon after your engagement party?"

"Frankly, I don't care." Kyle twisted his mouth. "But what about you, honey? Does it really matter to you so much what other people might think?"

His blunt words cut a sharp trail to her heart. "Of course not," she declared. "You misunderstand me, Kyle Hamilton. I don't care at all."

"Good," he said with almost smug satisfaction. "In that case, I'll pick you up at eight o'clock."

"You look very lovely, my dear," Andrew Wilkerson observed from his bed with a big smile. "Just like your mother."

"Thank you, Dad," Ashli replied in surprise. She'd never expected that simply dressing up in one of Helene's outfits would bring such an expression of delight to her father's face. The elderly man actually seemed to glow.

"Now *that's* the way I like to see my daughter dress," he remarked. "Don't you agree, Charles?"

"Most definitely," the butler replied, nodding. Actually, it had been Charles who had chosen the dress Ashli was wearing tonight from the extensive array of designer creations left abandoned in Helene's mirrored closets. As he always had since her childhood, the incredibly efficient butler had come to Ashli's rescue once more.

"How can I go anywhere elegant with Kyle?" she had confessed helplessly to Charles just an hour before, after having taken critical stock of her own neglected closets. "I forgot how unsuitable all my old clothes are." It was the sad truth. Ashli hadn't refurbished her wardrobe in five years, except for jeans, sweaters and T-shirts. Her expensive but hopelessly out-of-date dresses had all been chosen and worn when she was a high school girl. "I'm not seventeen years old anymore."

Charles had nodded grimly, then disappeared for several minutes into Helene's powder-blue bedroom suite. He emerged shortly afterward, carrying a delicate wisp of emerald green silk and sequins suspended from a padded hanger. "Your sister impetuously bought this gown last year, then decided she didn't care for it, after all. I think it would be most suitable for you, Miss Ashli."

"Do you really?" She fingered the elegant material with awe. It truly was exquisite—a glimmering jewel of a dress, with a plunging neckline, spaghetti straps and swirling hem which ended just above the knee. "You don't think it's too—daring?"

"Certainly not," the middle-aged butler insisted gently. "It's just that you haven't dressed up in a very long time."

Ashli gave a wistful sigh. To hear that tone in Charles's voice, she might have been nine years old again. How many countless other times had this stern-faced but kindly man nursed and encouraged her through a seemingly endless series of life's little crises? "I still don't feel right leaving Dad alone tonight."

"He is not alone," Charles reminded her with faint reproof. "I've been looking after your father for over thirty years, and can assure you he will be in excellent hands. Not to mention the fact that Jonas Hamilton will be returning later as well."

As always, it was impossible to argue with Charles Wingate. With a resigned sigh, Ashli had returned to her own room, taken an invigorating shower, and nervously prepared for her date with Kyle. How strange it felt, after all this time, to apply makeup. To brush her glossy, brown hair into a sophisticated style—swept up on one side with a jeweled comb, and left loose and flowing on the other side. To slip on sheer stockings and high heels. To feel the softness of silk against her skin. And then, once Ashli had finished dressing completely, to be met with an approving smile from her fastidious father.

"You look a movie star," he observed, beaming with delight.

"No, Dad," she protested. "Helene is the glamourous one in the family, don't you remember?"

"You're every bit as glamourous when you bother to take an ounce of trouble, my dear."

Ten minutes later, she walked self-consciously down the staircase to greet Kyle. As usual, he looked devastatingly attractive in a white dinner jacket, black tie and matching black slacks.

"Hello, Kyle," she greeted him shyly. Lord, how the man caused those butterflies to flutter in her stomach!

Kyle said nothing at first. For what seemed like an eternity, he simply stood there in silence, just staring at Ashli from head to toe. "You're the most beautiful thing I've ever seen," he declared at last. "Just look

at you, Ashli Wilkerson. What a glorious creature you
are.''

There was no doubting the raw sincerity in his
astonished voice, and it made Ashli tremble. "Thank
you," she answered with a tinge of embarrassment.

"You're not used to compliments, are you?"

Ashli nervously adjusted the spaghetti strap along
the bare skin of her shoulder. "No."

"Well, get used to it." Kyle's eyes glimmered a rare
silvery blue, as he leaned over and planted a brief,
tingling kiss on her soft mouth. "You really are
something," he added almost under his breath.

Ashli tried to ignore the hammering of her heart. "I
just hope you don't expect much at the club," she said,
attempting to sound casual. "I'm not a very good
dancer, in case you didn't know." *Unlike the graceful, nimble-footed Helene.*

"As far as expectations go," the handsome man in
the perfectly cut white dinner jacket said, smiling en-
igmatically, "all of mine have already been ex-
ceeded... by a long shot." Without another word, he
held open the front door for Ashli and they walked in
silence down to the driveway and Kyle's waiting white
sports car.

It had been years since Ashli had spent a Saturday
evening at the Elm Grove Country Club. On this particular August night, the air was balmy and a popular
dance orchestra played the strains of a familiar ballad
by Gershwin. Just as she remembered, there was the
elaborate dinner buffet crowned with a beautiful ice

sculpture, which tonight was a soaring crystalline swan. Unfortunately, just as Ashli had expected, there were also numerous curious glances from the club regulars. She blushed crimson beneath her golden tan.

"Ashli," Kyle said, placing a steadying arm around her waist as the maître d' led them to their table, "are you going to chicken out on me?" His voice was gently teasing.

"I'm not chickening out!" she whispered harshly. "But I knew this would happen. Everybody is staring at us!"

"Why not?" He grinned lightheartedly. "We're a great-looking couple."

She rolled her eyes. "Very funny, Kyle Hamilton! You know very well why they're all looking this way!" Ashli sat down, feeling distinctly uncomfortable, and began fidgeting with the linen dinner napkin. It seemed to her that everyone else in the elegant room had been guests at her sister's engagement party.

Kyle leaned back in his chair and lit a cigarette. "I admit that there are quite a few people right now who are dying with curiosity about the two of us, Ashli." He shrugged imperturbably. "They'll all find out soon enough, though."

"This doesn't bother you at all?" Ashli could still feel the sharp stare of the elderly couple at the next table. Why did they have to go out to the club this evening? Why couldn't Kyle just have taken her to a hamburger stand or something?

"No, it doesn't bother me," Kyle responded quietly. He nodded at the waiter, who popped open the waiting bottle of French champagne that had been chilling in a silver ice bucket before their arrival. After the champagne was poured, Kyle raised his glass to Ashli's. "Let's drink to Andrew's speedy recovery, and to our wedding, Ashli."

In mute assent, she lifted her crystal flute to Kyle's, and sipped some of the golden liquid. Immediately, her body began to tingle with a warm glow.

Kyle set down his glass. "There's something we need to discuss."

Ashli continued to sip her champagne. "What?"

For the first time all evening, he actually seemed a bit uneasy. "Ashli," Kyle began hesitantly, "I don't believe in long engagements."

"In case you think I've forgotten," she replied cynically, "you and Helene were ready to break the sound barrier."

"This isn't about Helene," he insisted, staring at her intently. "This is about *us,* Ashli."

"What about us?"

"I want to get married as soon as possible."

Ashli gazed back at him in bewilderment. "Where's the fire?"

Kyle twisted his mouth. "Funny you should put it that way. The fact is, there's a fire all right."

"What are you talking about?"

His blue eyes narrowed. "You know very well what I'm talking about, honey." There was an awkward silence. "Why don't we dance?"

Surprised at the quick way Kyle had changed the subject, Ashli gave a mental shrug. All that talk about women being the mysterious sex was totally absurd. Men were far more complicated and unpredictable. "I've already told you, I'm not a very good dancer."

"As it happens, I am very good...so it'll even out," he assured her. Not waiting for an answer, Kyle merely stood up and extended his hand. Ashli gave a reluctant sigh, and allowed herself to be led out onto the polished wood dance floor. In the past few days, she thought grimly, something had changed within her. After all those years of being feisty and independent, Kyle Hamilton had actually succeeded in rendering her almost docile. And after all this time of being a loner, Ashli was completely unprepared for the high-handed way this man had managed to rein her in. He seemed so confident, so at ease with himself. Ashli found herself feeling just a little resentful. Kyle was the kind of man who always seemed to get exactly what he wanted. With scarcely any effort at all. Look how easily *she* had yielded to him. She had fallen into his arms and accepted his proposal, just as she had allowed herself to drift into his arms out on the dance floor. But it was hard to deny the exquisite languor that once again engulfed her senses as Kyle held her body closely against his.

"You lied, Ashli," he whispered huskily into her ear.

"What are you talking about?"

"You said you weren't a good dancer."

"I'm not." Yet, strangely, every pore of Ashli's being seemed attuned to Kyle's movements. With gentle ease, he guided her across the small dance floor. The motion was slow but fluid. For the first time in her life, Ashli actually felt graceful instead of feeling as if she had two left feet. So, this was what is was like to be with the perfect dance partner. She gave an involuntary sigh and rested her cheek against the fine silk of Kyle's dress shirt. Through the thin material, his muscular warmth was undeniable. It was intoxicating to feel him in such an intimate way. The heat of his hands burned into her waist and the bare skin of her back.

"Believe me," he practically groaned, "you're doing just fine." The sensation of Ashli's slender, soft body pressed so closely against his, intoxicated Kyle. To have her like this, so sweet and yielding in his arms on the dance floor, was almost an almost unbearable pleasure. In fact, it was taking every ounce of willpower he could muster not to start beaming like some contented, moonstruck idiot. And that sexy little green wisp of a dress that Ashli was wearing tonight actually revealed more of her delectable figure than it concealed. Kyle had been completely stunned when he'd first caught sight of her this evening. Of course, he had expected Ashli to look beautiful the first time he'd seen her in a dress—but Kyle hadn't been prepared to be knocked on his ear the way he had been. "That's quite a dress you're *not* wearing," he added hoarsely.

"I'll have you know that Charles himself selected this dress for me," Ashli tossed back defensively.

"I find that hard to believe."

She tried to ignore the hammering of her heart as Kyle's hands travelled slowly down to the base of her spine in a blatantly possessive gesture. "Uh, it's true. This gown used to be Helene's," Ashli stammered with another self-conscious blush.

Kyle paused. "I only know that on you, Ashli, that dress should be registered as a deadly weapon."

"Deadly to whom?"

"To *any* red-blooded male."

"I assume that's supposed to be a compliment."

"Oh, it's a compliment, all right. Believe me." With a bemused sigh, Kyle drew her even more tightly against this powerful frame, and Ashli became aware of his frank arousal. The effect was shattering. Completely of her own volition, she reached up and wound her arms around Kyle's neck. "Ashli!" he exclaimed in astonished delight.

"What?" It was dizzying to feel his immediate shudder and realize that she could have such a powerful effect on a man. After years of denying her womanhood, it thrilled Ashli to know she had such an impact on Kyle Hamilton—the one person she had always believed to be so totally inaccessible.

But just at that moment, the music came to an end, and with a cold splash of reality, Ashli remembered where they both were. On the very public dance floor of the Elm Grove Country Club. And the hushed whispers and surprised stares of everyone else in the room—friends, acquaintances and strangers, served as a painful reminder that there was no privacy in a small town. By tomorrow, she and Kyle would be the

main topic of discussion over practically every breakfast table in town. Just another juicy tidbit of gossip
in the local rumor mill. Suddenly queasy, she pulled
away from Kyle's possessive grasp and headed back to
the table.

He was beside her in two long strides. "What is it?"

Ashli gave a pained sigh. "Do you really have to ask
that question?"

"Yes," he admitted tensely. "Just a moment ago,
you and I were having a great time." He twisted his
mouth. "At least, I thought we were."

She couldn't bring herself to sit down. "Just look
around, Kyle. It's like being in a goldfish bowl."

He followed the path of her embarrassed eyes, and
noted the curious glances that seemed to zoom from
everywhere. "I'm sorry," Kyle apologized quietly. "I
didn't notice until now."

"Are you serious?"

He grimaced. "Let's just say I was distracted."
There was an uncomfortable silence. "I guess this
wasn't a very wise idea."

She felt suddenly apologetic, too. "You were right
before, Kyle. I *was* having a good time."

He gazed at her thoughtfully. "Let's get out of here,
honey."

Kyle didn't have to ask twice. There were even more
curious glances as they walked from the room. Several times, they were accosted by friends who inquired about Andrew. Ashli answered their queries
with her characteristic warmth, but beneath the sur-

face, she was well aware of the real question on everyone's mind: *Where was Helene?*

Once again outside in the balmy night air, they walked silently across the gravel toward Kyle's white convertible. It wasn't until she was leaning back against the soft red leather upholstery, that Kyle shook his head. "Hell," he muttered, turning on the ignition, "that was a stupid, insensitive thing to do. I apologize, Ashli."

"It's all right. Just forget it," she said blithely.

"I can't forget it." He threw the car into gear, and the sleek machine screeched noisily down the driveway. "The truth is, I was being selfish. I wanted everyone to know about us."

She turned abruptly to stare at his taut profile against the flickering shadows of the moonlit sky. "Why?"

"Why?" His voice echoed harshly. "I was thinking about your reputation, Ashli."

Her lips quivered. "Excuse me?"

Kyle's hard, tanned fingers tightened on the steering wheel. "You find that hard to believe, don't you?" he asked.

"I never said that."

"It doesn't matter. I can read you like a book." He shook his head wearily. "I thought I was doing the right thing. I didn't want to wait until news got out about Helene running away with another man. I thought if people saw the two of us together *now,* they wouldn't get the wrong idea later on down the road."

The night breeze rushing through the open convertible fluttered Ashli's brown hair. "I don't understand."

Kyle's face was bleak, unsmiling. "You could be the focus of unwanted attention."

"I thought I already was."

"Tonight wasn't the same thing." For the first time, Kyle actually seemed at a loss for words. "Ashli, I don't want anyone to get the mistaken impression that I was marrying you on the rebound."

Her heart gave a hopeful twinge. "What are you trying to say?" Was it possible that Kyle had deeper feelings than he had previously revealed? Or was that just a phantom dream?

"The truth is," he went on matter-of-factly, "you and I are far better-suited to each other than Helene and I were."

Wishful thinking. Ashli gave a silent, bitter laugh. Kyle would be a tender, passionate and generous husband, but he could never love her. Why was this realization more painful than the years of frustration and heartache she had suffered as a result of her attachment to Edward? Why was she suddenly feeling so unsatisfied and miserable? Surely, being desired by Kyle Hamilton could be sweet enough. After all, love wasn't everything. Why reach for the moon when she could keep her feet firmly on the ground?

Ashli was so absorbed in these thoughts, that she barely realized the car had come to a stop. To her sheer astonishment, she saw that they had pulled into the driveway not of her home, but instead, the Hamilton estate. She stared at the rambling, white Victorian structure for a moment. It gleamed like a giant ivory cameo against the dark August sky. "What are we doing here?"

Kyle eyed her steadily. "It was the only place I could think of where we could have some privacy. I guarantee nobody will stare at us here. Or gossip."

"Oh."

He seemed to sense her inner tension. "Honey, I just figured we needed a place where we could relax and be ourselves...away from prying eyes." He looked into her eyes. "I'm not going to try to seduce you."

His last remark left Ashli feeling strangely deflated. Quickly, she opened the passenger door and remarked, "I'd like to use your phone to see how Dad is doing."

Kyle noted her flustered voice but made no comment. "Sure, let's go into the study and call Charles and Jonas."

Numbly, she followed him up the steps to the elegant porticoed entrance. Ashli had completely forgotten that Jonas was visiting with Andrew tonight. Kyle fumbled for a moment with his keys as he unlocked the exquisite oak and beveled glass front door and led the way through the wide, carpeted center hall toward the richly paneled study. *She and Kyle were alone together in the house.* A million warning bells should be going off in her brain, but oddly, Ashli felt no fear at all. If anyone seemed nervous, it was Kyle, himself.

"Would you care for some brandy?" he asked in a subdued tone.

"No, thank you." Ashli perched herself on the arm of the burgundy leather sofa, and dialed the telephone. Talking to Charles, she was totally unaware of Kyle's intense blue gaze on her legs. The cutaway hem of the green silk skirt had parted above the knee to reveal the feminine curve of one thigh. Shakily, Kyle poured himself a drink from the cut crystal decanter, and gulped it down.

Meanwhile, Ashli was busy listening to the butler on the other end of the receiver. Andrew was just fine, he said, and was sitting up in bed playing poker with Jonas. Apparently, Helene had called to have a heart-to-heart conversation with her father. She and Simon had been married this morning by a justice of the peace in Bennington. They would be driving down for the Labor Day weekend, so that Simon could meet the family.

Ashli placed her hand over the mouthpiece. "Helene's married," she said glancing at Kyle.

"Good," he responded with a cynical nod.

But now the serene expression abruptly faded from Ashli's face as Charles gave her another phone message. "*Who* called me?"

Kyle arched an eyebrow as he observed the change in Ashli.

"Well, what did *he* want?" she asked tartly.

Edward DePaul had called and left her a message.

Kyle listened silently, and set his drink down on the bar. He waited for Ashli to hang up the receiver, and regarded the two bright spots of pink that suffused her cheeks. "So," he remarked after a moment, "who called your house while we were out?"

"It's not important," she said evasively.

Kyle loosened his tie and took several steps toward her. "Oh, I'm sure it must have been important, to make you blush, Ashli." His tone was almost accusing.

"It was nobody..." she said, shaking her head. "Look, it isn't important, because it doesn't matter anymore." It was the truth, of course. Edward had made a concerned, friendly phone call to inquire if Ashli really had no intention of returning to California to assist him on his latest research project in the fall. If so, it would be a bitter disappointment. She was such an able, irreplaceable friend. But the crumbs of friendship were something that Ashli no longer had any desire to settle for. She needed to be wanted as a *woman*. Nothing or no one that existed before Kyle mattered to Ashli anymore. All that mattered was being with the man she loved.

Kyle exhaled raggedly. "It was that professor of yours, wasn't it?"

Ashli shrugged. "Look, I already told you it doesn't matter."

"Why not?" He took several steps closer.

"Because..." Embarrassed, Ashli turned her head away and folded her arms. "Just take my word for it."

Kyle hovered over her. "He wants you back, doesn't he?"

"Must we talk about this?"

"You bet we do," he growled harshly. "That egg-head wimp calls and you jump. I'll just bet you'll be heading back to Los Angeles on the first flight you can get!"

Ashli's hazel eyes widened in amazement. She had never seen Kyle this way before. She hadn't thought it was possible that a man so confident and handsome could actually be jealous. But the dark fury on his face was unmistakable. "Kyle Hamilton," she said slowly, "are you jealous?"

Roughly, he grasped her arms and pulled her up from the sofa. "Damn right, I'm jealous!" His voice was scorching. "How can you run back to another man when you belong to me?"

The possessive mastery in his words caused a delicious shiver up Ashli's spine, but stubbornly she retorted, "I don't belong to any man, least of all, to you. I'm a free and independent human being."

"You belong to me," Kyle insisted gruffly, "and I belong to you. How can you deny what happens when we touch each other?"

His hard fingers burned into her tingling flesh. There was no concealing the goosebumps along her bare, slender arms. "I'm not denying it," she stammered helplessly.

His eyes glittered down at hers. "Well, then, perhaps actions will speak louder than words."

Chapter Ten

The burning heat in his words made Ashli shudder. "What do you mean?"

Kyle's finger traced a tantalizing line from the green spaghetti strap at her shoulder toward the plunging of the silk and sequined neckline. "Don't be naive, honey. You know exactly what I'm talking about!" He leaned over suddenly and pressed his mouth along the base of Ashli's throat. "We're completely alone in the house." He paused significantly. "Why should we wait any longer?"

"Kyle!" Now his meaning had become utterly clear. Ashli was shocked.

"Oh, don't look so scandalized!" he taunted gently. "It isn't necessary to play the outraged virgin with me, Ashli." Kyle didn't wait for a reply, but scooped her up in his arms and deposited her in the center of the sofa. Impatiently, he tugged off his expensive dinner jacket and threw it down on the carpet.

"Wait a minute!" Ashli backed away as Kyle joined her on the leather cushions. "You don't understand!"

"Oh, I understand perfectly," Kyle replied in a thick voice. "The time for talk is over, darling. Actions speak much louder than words. Let me show you how much I want you." He pulled her up against his hard length, the heat of his muscular thighs evident through the fine material of his dress trousers.

There was no time for any further protest as Kyle's mouth claimed hers. Now, there was a new urgency to his touch, almost a desperation, as his hands traveled downward over the thin silk of her dress to grasp her hips and mold them against his own. There was a new kind of boldness, a new kind of daring intimacy in his caress. As Kyle's mouth found little resistance in Ashli's soft, tender mouth, he pushed her lips apart to taste the sweetness within with his greedy tongue.

"Say you don't want this," he breathed hotly against the sensitive column of her throat.

"I want it," she whispered timidly. "Please, touch me Kyle!"

Kyle groaned, "Yes, honey. I'll touch you everywhere." His mouth descended hungrily to ravage her lips, her cheeks, her throat with increasing ardor. Any further resistance to Kyle's sensual onslaught was washed away as Ashli melted beneath the persuasiveness of his expert kisses. She planted tiny butterfly kisses of her own along Kyle's eyelids and the corners of his hard mouth.

"Yes, sweetheart," Kyle gasped. "Touch me, too."

Ashli reveled in the fresh scent of him, his very maleness. She ran her fingers through his short, vibrant blond hair, enjoying the sweet accessibility of him. He gave another groan of pleasure when Ashli pressed her gentle lips against the tiny vein throbbing in the sinewy cord of his neck.

"You're delectable, honey," he ground out against the tender flesh of her earlobe. "Come here." Kyle's hands moved daringly up from her hips to cup the rounded softness of each breast.

"Kyle!" she exclaimed in a half whisper.

"Do you like that?" he asked softly as he continued his exploration of Ashli's sweet fullness, slipping one urgent hand inside the plunging neckline of her evening dress.

She suppressed a shudder as his fingers gently brushed the tip of her breast and teased the point to hardness. No man had ever touched her so intimately before. She felt wild and out of control, but the last thing on earth Ashli wanted at this very moment, was for Kyle to stop his maddeningly delicious caresses.

"You're like velvet and silk in my hands, honey," he rasped. Kyle was completely out of control now, and he knew it. But tonight, he had no intention of stopping this sweet seduction until it was over. Sure, knowing fingers found the zipper in the back of Ashli's dress, and in another moment, the spaghetti straps were being pulled down to her waist, revealing the creamy bareness of her breasts.

"Oh!" she exclaimed, instinctively crossing her arms in a protective gesture.

"No, darling," Kyle whispered hoarsely. "Let me see how beautiful you are." With infinite gentleness, he pushed her arms away and gazed down at her exposed flesh. "So perfect, so beautiful," he murmured deeply. "How could I have been so stupid to have waited this long to touch you?" A deliberate finger traced a tingling line from the tips of both breasts. Two firm hands gripped the swelling mounds with gentle pressure, readying them for the descent of his mouth. Ashli moaned with pleasure as Kyle's eager lips claimed one of the firm pink nipples, flicking his tongue over the silky, hardened bud. Time lost all meaning as Kyle willed Ashli to respond to the raging fire within him. She was pulled down into a vortex of passion from which there could be no turning back.

"I want you so badly, I ache inside," he growled heavily, as he continued to pull away the wispy silk dress, down past her hips, her thighs, until it lay tossed in a crumpled heap on the carpet next to Kyle's discarded jacket. Boldly, he caressed the smooth columns of her thighs and pressed an intimate kiss on the satiny bareness of Ashli's flat stomach. "You're so lovely, so perfect!" He devoured her with narrowed eyes, and touched the lacy waistband of her pink bikini panties. "I'll make it wonderful for you, darling. So wonderful that you'll forget all about that professor of yours."

Ashli shivered with delicious anticipation, as Kyle turned away briefly to remove his shirt and tie. It was going to happen, she thought with dazed wonderment. In a few moments, Kyle would possess her completely and she would finally learn the aching secrets of sexual fulfillment. It would all be perfect and beautiful because she loved this man with all her heart and soul. And even though he didn't feel the same way, Ashli realized it was important to her that Kyle know. Know that he was loved and cherished enough to receive a woman's sweetest gift.

"Kyle," she breathed as he came back to her and held her against his bare, muscular chest.

"Yes, baby," he groaned in husky approval. "Say my name like that again. I go crazy when you say it!"

"Kyle—"

"Yes!" He arched her soft body up against his supple male strength.

"I want you to make love to me."

"I fully intend to, right at this very moment," he informed her in a thick voice.

"Just show me what to do," she pleaded softly. "Just show me what to do, Kyle!"

The man positioned above her on the leather couch suddenly froze. "What do you mean, 'show you'?"

She averted her eyes self-consciously. "I'm not sure how...I mean, the best way—" Ashli stopped. "It's just that I've never done this before and I don't want to make a fool of myself."

"You've never done *what* before?" Kyle's voice practically boomed.

She sighed. "Do I have to spell it out for you?"

Kyle's entire body shuddered. "Are you trying to tell me that this is your first time, Ashli?"

"Yes," she admitted simply.

"Oh, Lord!" He stared down at her in disbelief. "You mean to say that you're... you're a—"

She compressed her lips. "Don't say the word. Yes, I am, but just don't say that word."

"But after all these years—"

"I'm not *that* old."

Kyle's teeth clenched. "How can you still be a virgin?"

"I told you not to use that word!"

"Ashli," he groaned. "Don't you see how this changes things?"

"No."

"I thought that *surely* you and that professor friend of yours had—"

"We didn't." Why was Kyle so disturbed? She was baffled. Ashli had never expected he would respond this way.

Kyle gave a pained sigh and reached for his shirt. "I'd better take you home now."

"Take me home?" She looked at him with a wounded expression on her face. "Don't you want me anymore?"

"Oh, baby," he moaned, pulling her back into his arms and kissing the silky curve of her shoulder. "I want you so much that I can't stand it. But this isn't right. The first time it happens for you, I want it to be perfect...not some rushed, crazy moments on a sofa."

"But, Kyle—" she protested.

"Ssh." With a dark glitter in his eyes, Kyle pressed a gentle finger to her lips. "Whether you believe it or not, I am a gentleman, honey. And gentlemen have a code of honor about things like this." He paused. "Especially when they're..."

"When they're what?"

"Nothing," he replied hastily, and covered the exposed part of her body with the soft shirt.

What had he been about to say? she wondered. "Listen to me, Kyle," she implored.

A thought suddenly occurred to him now. A thought so new and unbelievable that Kyle was afraid to voice it aloud. "Ashli," he said, brushing the silky brown strands of hair out of her eyes. "Just answer me one question. Why were you so willing to give yourself to me after all these years of waiting?" He seemed truly troubled. "Why me? Why *now?*"

Ashli locked her brown gaze with his concerned blue eyes. Why hold any more secrets from the man? What was the point? "Because I love you, Kyle," she replied simply.

For a moment, he seemed at a loss for words. "What did you say?"

"I'm in love with you, Kyle Hamilton. You might as well know it, even though I realize you don't feel the same way." She stared at him bravely. "It's all right, though."

His jaw practically dropped. "You really love me?" Kyle gave a groan, and pulled her back into his powerful embrace. "You've tortured me all this time, and

I never knew you cared." He drew a deep breath. "Here I thought I was just a jerk in love with a woman who was carrying the torch for another man."

Ashli swallowed convulsively. "You *love* me?"

"Yes, sweetheart." He looked at her with tenderness. "I've loved you since that first moment on the staircase. I knew I had to have you, no matter what the consequences."

She gave a sigh of contentment and buried her cheek in Kyle's muscular shoulder. "I can't believe you really love me."

Kyle twisted his lips in a faint smile. "You just wait until our wedding night, darling, and I'll prove to you how much I love you."

Daringly, Ashli ran a gentle finger across his chest. "Do we really have to wait?"

"Tomorrow isn't such a long time," Kyle murmured with a silky laugh, as he pulled his dress shirt tighter around Ashli's shoulders and hugged her tenderly.

*   *   *   *   *

This is the season of giving, and Silhouette proudly offers you its sixth annual Christmas collection.

SILHOUETTE

Christmas Stories

1991

Experience the joys of a holiday romance and treasure these heartwarming stories by four award-winning Silhouette authors:

> Phyllis Halldorson—"A Memorable Noel"
> Peggy Webb—"I Heard the Rabbits Singing"
> Naomi Horton—"Dreaming of Angels"
> Heather Graham Pozzessere—"The Christmas Bride"

Discover this yuletide celebration—sit back and enjoy Silhouette's Christmas gift of love.

Take 4 bestselling love stories FREE

Plus get a FREE surprise gift!

Special Limited-time Offer

Mail to Silhouette Reader Service™

In the U.S.	In Canada
3010 Walden Avenue	P.O. Box 609
P.O. Box 1867	Fort Erie, Ontario
Buffalo, N.Y. 14269-1867	L2A 5X3

YES! Please send me 4 free Silhouette Romance® novels and my free surprise gift. Then send me 6 brand-new novels every month, which I will receive months before they appear in bookstores. Bill me at the low price of $2.25* each—a savings of 34¢ apiece off cover prices. There are no shipping, handling or other hidden costs. I understand that accepting the books and gift places me under no obligation ever to buy any books. I can always return a shipment and cancel at any time. Even if I never buy another book from Silhouette, the 4 free books and the surprise gift are mine to keep forever.

*Offer slightly different in Canada—$2.25 per book plus 69¢ per shipment for delivery. Canadian residents add applicable federal and provincial sales tax. Sales tax applicable in N.Y.

215 BPA ADL9   315 BPA ADMN

Name _____ (PLEASE PRINT)

Address _____ Apt. No. _____

City _____ State/Prov. _____ Zip/Postal Code _____

This offer is limited to one order per household and not valid to present Silhouette Romance® subscribers. Terms and prices are subject to change.

SROM-91   © 1990 Harlequin Enterprises Limited

DONAVAN
Diana Palmer

Diana Palmer's bestselling LONG, TALL TEXANS series continues with DONAVAN....

From the moment elegant Fay York walked into the bar on the wrong side of town, rugged Texan Donavan Langley knew she was trouble. But the lovely young innocent awoke a tenderness in him that he'd never known...and a desire to make her a proposal she couldn't refuse....

Don't miss DONAVAN by Diana Palmer, the ninth book in her LONG, TALL TEXANS series. Coming in January...only from Silhouette Romance. LT192